DESERT FIRE

A Novel

By

Stoney Livingston

Stoney Livingston

ISBN-13:978-0692447673
ISBN-10:0692447679

This is a work of fiction

Cover by Terry Del Bene

Desert Fire

CHAPTER ONE

U.S. Marine Captain James Campbell hit the ejection lever only three seconds before the Iraqi ground missile blew his F-18 Hornet into a ball of flame and smoke. The immediate rush of air as the canopy shot skyward created a momentary vacuum. The sudden change in pressure caused his ears to pop and he felt his heart thump twice like a lead hammer in his chest. Then the ejection charges under his seat blasted him upward and out of the plane.

The force of his exploding F-18 below him hurled Campbell upward an additional hundred yards before gravity took over and started him tumbling earthward. He felt dizzy and nauseous. There was no frame of reference in the darkness. He wasn't sure if he was falling or ascending. Tracers flew by him in the night and they came from the direction he thought was up. His mind raced for explanations and searched for salvation at the same time. Where was he? Too many unanswered questions. He felt consciousness slipping away. His chute opened and he was jolted by the sudden slowing of his fall. He drifted earthward below his billowed parachute.

The concrete floor was cold on his cheek. His body ached all over. Campbell opened his eyes slowly and surveyed his surroundings as completely as possible without moving. Even the movement of his eyelids caused him pain.

The memory of an exploding Iraqi MIG-29 flashed through his brain. The ejection. *Where the hell is Ed? He never should have followed me down that low. Hell, I shouldn't have gone that low myself. Sweet Jesus, I hope he got out. Second day of this damn Iraqi war and I'm out of action. I'll bet Ed is really bent out of shape.* He couldn't remember seeing his wingman's plane when he had ejected.

The room was empty of furniture, the interior walls bare concrete, stark and impenetrable. He became aware his hands were tied behind his back and knew he had been captured. With that realization came first the fear, then the imperative: he had to escape. *Damn! I've really done it this time. Bob's gonna have my ass for dropping so low for that MIG. I got him with the Vulcan cannon, not a missle. That ought to be worth something. I lost my plane and now these ragheads have got a bonafide American pilot to parade around. I let everybody down – my buddies – my country – the Corps. Somehow I don't feel like such a hero now.*

A voice above and behind him slammed into his consciousness, the words and sounds unfamiliar, almost surreal. He kept his eyes open without moving or responding, mentally tallying his injuries, finding to the best of his knowledge that none were serious. He felt pain from minor lacerations and bruises, mostly in his chest, and he was aware of a stinging cut on his right forearm. His head throbbed incessantly but there seemed to be no broken bones. *Give me half a chance. That's all I want. Just half a chance. I'll bust out of here so fast, you won't even know I was ever here.*

A second voice sounded, this one slightly higher than the first. The first speaker answered, then addressed Campbell in English. "What is your name?" The words were chopped.

Campbell's lips were dry. The long flight from his carrier to the target and his ejection from the plane and subsequent exposure to the dryness of the desert air had left him dehydrated. He pulled his cheek from the cement floor, rolled onto his back and sat up, facing the speaker, the maneuver made difficult with his hands tied behind his back. The smaller man, the one with the higher voice, held an AK-47 at the ready. *Goddamn. This is for real. How do I play this? I can't show too much fear – a little maybe – enough to be respectful – but not too much.* "Y'all got any watah?" he whispered.

The unarmed Iraqi kicked him in the chest. Campbell fell back onto the cold concrete, avoiding a broken skull only by rolling with the force of the blow as he had learned to do in boot camp.

He painfully sat back up and grinned at his captors. "Have a rough naht, did ya?"

The bigger of the two men, the one with the deeper voice and some sort of medal on his brown uniform, hovered over him menacingly. "What is your name, American?"

Campbell smiled and again put on his Deep South accent. "Ah'm sorry. Ah didn't quaht get a fihm grip on what it was y'all said."

The two captors exchanged glances. The bigger one turned back to him. "I ask your name," he glowered.

"Why shucks, ah'm sorry. It's Jim." Campbell grinned again. "What's y'all's?"

The big man smashed him in the cheek with a closed fist.

Campbell again fell to the floor, his brain reeling with pain. He sat up slowly and stared at his captors, the smile gone from his face. He resisted the impulse to leap at the Iraqi with the rifle, tied hands or no tied hands. He knew he would get only one chance, if he were lucky. It had to wait until he knew more about his situation, and his hands were free. He stared into the eyes of the bigger man. "Ah'm taard uv playin' games w' y'all. Ah'm Captain James J. Campbell."

The big man smiled. "It is good you cooperate, Captain Campbell."

"How 'bout that wahtah?" Campbell didn't know how long he could keep up his southern accent. He wasn't sure why yet, but he felt it was important to maintain the charade. *I'm gonna put one over on you assholes. Somehow I'm gonna do it.* Concentrating on the structure of the words took his mind away from some of the pain and lessened his desire to do something foolish.

"Of course. But first we must know certain questions."

"Then ah'm afraid ah'm gonna have to stay thusty, 'cause y'all just got all the cooperation outa me y'all 're gonna git."

Again the big man struck him in the face with a fist. Campbell maintained his sitting position, even as he felt the blood trickling down his cheek and experienced the metallic taste of blood. "Now, Captain, we talk. What is the unit?"

Campbell stared hard into the bigger man's eyes, wishing he could bore into his brain and kill him with the power of his mind. It didn't work. *If my hands weren't tied you wouldn't have the balls to politely say "hello" to me, you chickenshit sonofabitch.* "Ah'd sure appreciate it if y'all'd take out a pencil and a piece of papuh and write this heah infomation down, 'cause ah'm gittin' tarred uv repeatin' it. Captain James J. Campbell. And since the Geneva Conventions don't seem tah mean much to y'all, that's all yer gonna git." Campbell took no small pleasure in not complying with his requirements under the Geneva Conventions. They were going to beat him anyway; why give them his serial number and date of birth?

He saw the blow coming and was able to lessen its impact by rolling his head at the last second. *That could be considered a pretty good reason to give 'em my serial number and date of birth.* The blood flow increased down his cheek. He could taste it in the corner of his mouth.

"What is the unit?"

Campbell grinned again and said, "*No comprende.*"

He felt the impact of a rifle butt on the side of his head with enough force to cause a flash of bright light in his brain as he collapsed to the floor. The bigger man kicked him in the ribs and face, then pulled his head up, using his hair as a handle. Blood spurted from Campbell's nose and mouth. The Iraqi smiled. "Let me I tell you thees wan. You not so tough now, eh, Captain?"

Campbell returned the smile with a bloody one of his own. "You know, y'all are beginnin' ta piss me off."

The Iraqi smashed him in the face with a clenched fist. A greyness engulfed Campbell but he fought it off. He feared what they might do to him while he was unconscious. He spit out a small chip from one of his teeth. His mouth was so numb, he couldn't be sure which tooth it came from. He looked up at the larger man, then at the smaller. The crooked smile on the little man's face brought rage to Campbell's mind. He struggled for control.

"Y'all know who y'all remahnd me of? Howdy Doody. Ah sweah, if you hahd red haea, you'd be a deahd ringa." He grinned back to the bigger man. "And you theah, y'all remind me of Bozo. Both ah them fellas was clowns in theah own ways."

Bozo moved forward, his hand raised for another blow. A third man entered the room. "Enough!"

Campbell turned to face the newcomer. "Well, ah'll be damned. Now we got Doctor Kildahe."

Doctor Kildare wore a white lab coat and an apologizing smile. His polished black shoes glistened in the bright light of the exposed light bulb overhead. "I'm sorry. It was never our intention for them to go this far." His English was choppy.

Campbell smiled. He felt the blood in his mouth flow onto his chin and imagined a row of red teeth and bleeding gums. He shrugged. "Ah didn't etha, but ah wouldn't be too hahd on 'em, Doc. They was just enjoyin' theah work."

Kildare stepped next to him and knelt. He checked Campbell's pulse then looked into his eyes with the aid of a small penlight. "How do you feel?"

"Ah feel great, Doc. Me 'n' the boys was just fixin' tah go a couple moah rounds when y'all busted up the pahty."

"I am sorry about the other pilot."

Campbell felt a sinking sensation in his chest. "What ah y'all talkin' 'bout?"

Doctor Kildare's facial features softened. "The other pilot. He was killed resisting capture."

Campbell held a blank stare.

Kildare reached into a pocket of the lab coat and withdrew a needle and syringe. Campbell's eyes grew wide with fear. He knew it showed. *Jesus! You dirty sonofabitch. You rotten, dirty sonofabitch. I'd rather die with a bullet in my head. You're not prying any secrets out of me that way.* He leaned away from the doctor.

"Ah'm fine, Doc. No complaints heah. Whah don't you save that stuff for these boys afta ah next round?"

The smiling face moved closer. "It's a mild sedative and pain suppressant. I assure you, you have nothing to fear." He brought the needle close to Campbell's arm.

"Y'all don't listen too well, Doc." Campbell lost his composure. From his sitting position, he brought up a leg and kicked the syringe from the doctor's hand. The two guards pounced on him. One struck him in the face and chest, then grabbed his upper body, while the other pinned his legs to the concrete floor. The doctor retrieved the syringe from the floor and jammed it into Campbell's arm though the material of his flight suit.

Campbell felt the liquid enter his body and spread upward in a slow burn. He stared into the face of the man in the lab coat, only inches from his own. He wanted to kill him more than anything he had ever wanted in his life but he knew it was over. Fear gripped him; his stomach tightened into a knot. Whatever had been in that syringe was doing its work. If it was poison, he was dead. If it were something else, he would regain consciousness. He concentrated on a southern accent and a small town in northern Alabama. He blanked the rest of his past from his mind. He looked up at Bozo who had loosened his grip.

Desert Fire

"Yoah breath stinks, Bozo." His world went black.

Within seconds of regaining consciousness, Campbell realized he had been moved. He couldn't prove what he felt but the feeling was strong enough to convince him it was fact. The building in which he found himself didn't resemble any of the known targets in his sector of operation, nor was it a field concrete bunker like the one in which he'd met Howdy Doody and Bozo. It obviously had great military importance. He could see military and civilian personnel pass by the wire-reinforced window in the top half of the door to his room in a steady stream. He couldn't determine the functions performed, but operations and intelligence were logical candidates in his mind.

He was weak and spent. He lay on his back, unmoving, and looked at the back of a guard, who stood slightly to the side of the door outside his room. Many of the men he saw pass by the window appeared to be civilians. Campbell found that unusual in a country where almost every male wore a uniform.

The interior of his room was more comfortable than the one in which he had been beaten and drugged. A metal-framed bunk held a thin mattress covered by a drab blanket. There was no other furniture. Whatever the room had been designed for, it was not for the holding of prisoners. Although the interior wall was solid concrete, it had no toilet facilities. There were no provisions for passing food to a prisoner without opening the door completely, and the door itself was lacquered wood with a wire-reinforced glass window in the top half.

Campbell remained motionless for almost three hours. He listened and observed what he could of his environment, grateful for the respite from the beatings. After a time, he rolled onto his side and faced the wall, afraid the fear and shame written on his face would be read by his captors. His tongue reminded him of his chipped tooth. *What a waste. I let 'em all down. If only I could grab back that stupid second when I decided to go after that*

MIG. He stared at the wall. *I'm sorry, Ed.* Only the blank, grey wall bore witness to his silent tears.

He wiped his eyes and clamped his jaw tightly shut. *Screw you. You'll never beat me. That's enough of that self pity, Campbell. You're not the only guy who ever got captured and worked over a little bit. You can take anything these monkeys can hand out. Spit in their eyes. If they're going to take you out, don't give 'em any satisfaction beyond your death.* He searched the room, his eyes going over every square inch of the concrete. The only breaks in the even grey walls were the door and the light fixture overhead. *I wonder if they can hide a camera in a light bulb?* He wiped his eyes with an arm.

He rolled over and sat up facing the door. "Hey, raghead. Ah gotta pee."

The guard burst into the room and waved his rifle menacingly. "Stay!"

Campbell sat on the edge of the bunk. "Stay? Stay? That's all y'all 're gonna say? Ah'm talking ah serious bladder problem heah, and all y'all have to say is 'stay'?" Campbell pointed to his crotch.

The guard motioned him to wait and stepped out of the room, returning momentarily with a second man to escort him to the bathroom. They cuffed Campbell's hands in front of him and led him into the wide, dimly lit hallway. He waited for the guards to strike him but they kept their distance at three feet front and rear.

Warning signs flashed through Campbell's mind as he saw a section of the interior wall in the process of being modified. The center of the concrete, in addition to the standard rebar, contained a sheet of lead. The warning signs turned to bells and sirens as he glanced quickly down an intersecting hallway and glimpsed a sign, the international radioactive symbol, prominently displayed over an emergency showerhead. He looked quickly ahead, a dumb smile on his face. The leading guard turned and smiled just as dumbly back at him.

The bathroom was well equipped with ten or more urinals and toilets, and several shower stalls, but despite his repeated requests, he was not allowed to use the showers; his awareness of his need to clean his body grew with his first look in the mirror.

His over-regulation-length, jet-black hair was unkempt and matted with blood. The cuts and bruises on his face showed plainly, even those in the shadow of his high cheekbones. His lower lip was puffed and grotesquely purple on the right side of his mouth; it looked almost like a giant blood blister. *If this is the worst that happens, I can handle it.*

"Go now," said one of his guards.

"If Y'all don't mahnd, I'd lahk ta tidy up a bit – you know, wash mah hands an' such." He looked briefly at the guard, then shook his head. "No, ah don't suppose y'all do know much about that." He turned and followed the lead guard back to his room.

A man in a white lab coat was present when they entered. With him stood a general holding a swagger stick. Campbell smiled a painful smile. "Howdy, Gents. Ah'd offah y'all a cheah, but y'all caught me short."

"What kind of aircraft you fly?" asked the general.

"General, suh, that's classifahd infahmation." Campbell glanced quickly around the room, then winked the less swollen of his eyes. "But since y'all 're ah general, ah reckon ah can confide in ya." He leaned close to the Iraqi officer. "Keep this heah infomation quaht now, you heah?"

The general nodded, a crooked smile curling his lips. He took a step closer. Their faces were only inches apart.

"Ah was flyin' the latest production Pipah Cub on the mahket. Best money could bah."

The smile left the general's face, only to be replaced by drawn lips almost as purple as Campbell's. He slapped Campbell in the face with the swagger stick.

Campbell staggered back a step. *Don't lose it now.* He stood his ground. "A Pipah Cub is a damn fahn ayacraft. Ah'll have y'all know, ah shot down foah ah y'all's best fightahs befoah ah ran outta gas."

The general clenched and unclenched his fists. Campbell watched him regain control. *Damn! Had that bastard goin' for a while there.*

The general spoke softly, obviously having great difficulty controlling his anger. "Captain, we want basic information and soon you can make statement to world on television you have done wrong. You can apologize to the peoples of Iraq."

Campbell's jaw dropped. "Ah don't know what the hell y'all been smokin' theah, suh, but ah'd give serious consideration tah changin' brands. Yoah grandkids'll be older'n y'all befoah y'all heah that kinda tripe from me."

The general calmly turned to the man in the lab coat. "Doctor."

The little man pulled a needle and syringe from his coat pocket.

Oh shit! Talk about unfair! You rotten sonofabitch. No, goddamnit, it's "Y'all're ah a rotten sonofabitch". Don't lose the accent.

He felt the needle enter his arm, then the slow burn, a slight ringing in his ears, dizziness. The floor moved. *Fuck y'all.*

On his second day at the facility, as Campbell was escorted to the bathroom, he noticed open blinds on a window not far from the bathroom. His heart raced as he glanced through the window and discovered the outer room of a nuclear reactor lab. Several men in white lab coats passed through an inner door into the lab. Campbell noted the heavy door. He closed his eyes and took a mental picture.

The blinds on the next room were also open. Campbell looked at a large sector map of the Middle East, complete with colored pins and acetate cover. There were symbols of Allied aircraft, with large numbers next to them. *I wonder if that's sighted or shot down?* He doubted the allied losses could be as high as the numbers indicated. Again he closed his eyes momentarily, capturing the image in his mind.

What the hell are they doing, letting me see this stuff? He felt the fear growing in his stomach and spreading its way to his throat.

When he returned to his room there were two more uniformed soldiers; one of them wore the rank of general and carried a swagger stick. *Not this asshole again.*

"Good morning, Captain," said the general.

"It was," returned Campbell dryly.

The general struck him in the face with the swagger stick. Campbell flinched from the blow but remained standing.

The general's face turned beet red. "You will show respect for superiors!"

Campbell glanced quickly around the room. "Beggin' yoah pahdon, suh, but ah don't see anyone in heah that's superiah tah me."

Again the swagger stick struck him on the cheek. Campbell tasted the blood in his mouth. *Here we go again.*

Campbell held up well during his beatings, interrogations and drug sessions, which seemed unending, though more care was taken not to strike him in the face after the general had vented his frustrations. This wasn't done out of concern for his welfare, of this he was sure, but more for the sake of his appearance. He knew they had plans for him. He took great satisfaction in not giving his tormentors what they wanted.

Two days after his last meeting with the general, Campbell was moved to another room in the large facility.

During his walk down the corridors on the way to his new room, two Iraqis with lab coats walked past Campbell and his guards. They carried a large, uncovered wooden box. Inside, several smaller metallic boxes rode in a layer of Styrofoam. *Those can't be what I think they are.* He peered at the devices intently as they passed within inches of him. *Jesus Christ! They are! Nuke triggers! We weren't sure they had these things.* The dull, lead-coated little boxes were primitive compared to the ones used by the United States, but they were capable of setting off a nuclear reaction. He had seen this exact model in training. He closed his eyes briefly. *It's French! About the late seventies. This plant's making nuclear weapons!* He snapped his eyes shut for a brief second.

He tried to remain calm and stupid looking to the Iraqis as he passed another large room containing a nuclear reactor. *They must be so certain the drugs are keeping me semi-comatose, they'll let me see their deepest secrets. Why in the hell did they bring me here in the first place? Am I another one of Hussein's famous "human shields? Boy is that a laugh. My own squadron would blow this place to hell with my blessing if they knew where it was.* He didn't see the reactor but he knew it was there. The universal symbols were present everywhere. He didn't have to speak their language to know it. He also knew they had no plans of letting him live after they got whatever it was they wanted from him. He smiled dumbly at his guards.

As he walked through the door of his new room, the two-man guard detail gave him a house-warming party. One of them pushed him roughly at the metal bunk against the wall. Campbell careened off the bunk and into the face of the second guard, bouncing up enough to strike the unsuspecting man in the chin with his shoulder. As the guard fell back, Campbell kicked hard into the groin of the man who had pushed him. He felt his foot strike home. The stricken man screamed. *I should have known this was going to happen when they put my hands behind my back instead of cuffing me from the front. Damnit!*

Uniformed men rushed into the room as quickly as if they

had been standing by for such a happening. Campbell struggled but, without the use of his hands, he was quickly overcome. They pinned him to the floor and beat him in the ribs and stomach.

He forced himself to think of something else, to ignore the pain he couldn't stop anyway. He fantasized as they beat and kicked him. *I'll bust out and lead my squadron back here. Maybe Bob won't be so pissed off about my plane. That was a damn good plane. I'll get even for Ed.* The intensity of his concentration helped to lessen the pain. He remained conscious only out of determination.

A man in a white smock rushed into the room. Campbell stared at him and the syringe in his hand, his eyes wide. Two guards held his arms and legs. He struggled, grunting and trying to bite his captors but was unable to break free. He said nothing as he stared rays of hate at the man with the syringe.

Campbell felt the initial prick of the needle, then the warm glow of the drug; a fire spread through him, then a chill. *Oh, shit! What the hell is this? Something new. Oh, Christ. Think southern accent. Don't let 'em win this one. Alabama. Deep south. Southern fried chick. . .*

Early the next morning Campbell was marched into a spacious briefing room, his hands untied. His guards motioned to a chair and he sat down slowly, still weak from the effects of the unknown drug.

Three Iraqis sat facing him in front of a large sector map. One of them, the general with the swagger stick, pointed to a symbol of an aircraft carrier. "Captain Campbell, we know you flew from aircraft carrier. Is this location correct?" He tapped the map with his swagger stick.

Campbell leaned across the table and studied the map closely. He blinked his eyes and sharpened his focus. The Iraqis at the table smiled. Campbell let his eyes quickly glance at the local map to the right of the larger map. He noted a position marked with a red ink. *Damn, I wish I could read this lingo!* He blinked, sat back in his chair and glanced at the horizontal and vertical grids on the other map. A drunken smile worked its way across his lips.

"No."

The smiles of the Iraqis faded. "No?"

Campbell smiled up at the general. "No." He paused. "Ah hahd one ah them long-range ah'planes. Ah took off from a carrier in New York Habah. Hit a lot ah rough weathah on the way ovah heah too."

The swagger stick smashed into his upper arm with the sound of a clenched fist striking flesh. Campbell fell over backwards in his chair, mainly the result of his attempt at avoiding the blow. He crawled to his knees, hanging to the edge of his chair. "Y'all ain't heard the best paht yet. Mah plane got such good gas mileage, ah refueled ah buddy ah mahn who caught up with me on his way outa Califonia."

Two guards rushed from their positions at the door and wrestled him to the floor. They snapped handcuffs tightly around his wrists and lifted him to his feet by stretching his arms behind his back.

Campbell turned his head far enough to see one of them. "One ah these heah days ah'd lahk tah show y'all a few basic rules ah etiquette."

The other guard punched him in the ribs. They sat him roughly back into the chair. The general poked him in the chest. "Captain. Why are you so foolish? We know this information. We know which carrier you use."

Campbell ignored him. "Y'all know of coahse that y'all ain't got a snowball's chance in hell ah winnin' this heah wah. Whah don't y'all just surrender yoah swagger sticks to me and ah'll have mah boys go easy on y'all?"

The general's face tightened then relaxed as he regained control. "Do you think you are a tough guy, Captain Campbell?"

Desert Fire

Campbell put on his shy and hurt look. "Wah, no suh. Ah graduated last in mah class in boot camp. Mah nickname was 'Wimpy'. The really tough fellas will be comin' tah pay y'all a visit befoah this is ovah though. They only let me fly a mission tah make me feel bettah about mahself. Now ah'm in big trouble 'cause I only borrowed the ah'plane foah one day. Ah'm afraid it's past due. It's kinda lahk not returnin' ah library book on tahm. Them generals get real mad about things lahk. . . "

The swagger stick again. It caught him on the neck this time. He tumbled from the chair and crashed to the floor, able to protect his face only by turning his head.

The guards tossed him roughly back into the chair.

The general leaned across the table and put his face next to Campbell's. "I grow tired of your foolishness. If you do not cooperate, I will burn you like the American trash you are."

The welt caused by the swagger stick burned on Campbell's neck. "Vera well, suh. It seems y'all ah havin' ah difficult tahm undahstandin' that ah have no intention of cooperatin' with y'all, so ah'll try to put it a little moah succinctly -- fuck y'all, and the camel y'all rode in on."

The general's face turned beet red. He leaned away and shouted to the guards standing only three feet away. Campbell's heart leapt to his throat for the thousandth time since his capture. They grabbed him roughly by the arms and dragged him from the room, terror in his heart, but a smile on his face.

At the door to his room, one of the guards spit in his face. Campbell reacted without thinking. He hit the startled guard with a wad of spit right between the eyes. The guard wiped his face with his sleeve and waded into Campbell swinging. The second guard chattered loudly and pulled his indignant friend from the prisoner. They both pushed him into the room and slammed the door shut.

Campbell watched the two guards through the window in the door as they engaged in what appeared to him to be an

17

obvious and heated argument. *That's odd as hell. What's going on here?*

The following morning a man in a lab coat entered his room with two guards. Campbell recognized him. In his mind, he called the man Doctor Kildare but he hadn't bothered to speak it aloud. Kildare pulled out a syringe and looked sympathetically at his "patient." "I must ask you to sit on the bed." His grammar was quite correct, but his accent was as thick as his mustache.

Campbell held up a hand. One of the guards made a move towards him then held back. "See heah, Doctah. Ah don't see any moah need foah drugs. Y'all been askin' me tah make ah statement in front of ah television camera. If that's all y'all want, ah'll do it. Just don't give me anymoah ah them drugs."

The doctor nodded to the two guards. All three turned and left the room. Campbell sat on his bunk and waited. All of his life he had maintained hope, even in the most difficult of situations. Hope enabled him to get through boot camp. It put him through college. It made him a premier fighter pilot – first in his class at Pensacola. It had sustained his will to resist the Iraqis.

Hope was almost gone. His chances of making good on an escape were almost non-existent. No matter how short the war, the Allies wouldn't get to him in time to save his life. The constant beatings were taking a heavy toll on him physically. What little food he received was barely enough to sustain life under the most desirable of circumstances. And the strangeness of the food caused him mixed thoughts. He didn't know if the Iraqis ate food that tasted the way his did, or if his food were drugged. *You can do almost anything to rice.*

Kildare entered the room with the general who had beaten him in the arm and neck with his swagger stick. Campbell stood respectfully. *You may get me, you sonofabitch, but I'm gonna get you first, and you won't even know it until it's too late.*

The general smiled benignly. "I am told you will make a

statement. Why you changed your mind?"

"The drugs, Suh. It shoah as hell isn't because ah'm afraid of y'all beatin' me. Theah ain't a raghead alahve ah'm afraid of, and that includes y'all. It's the drugs.

"The drugs?" The general arched an eyebrow. "You are not so tough after all, huh?"

"Ah don't cayah what y'all think of me puhs'naly, but mah fathah is mahty sick. Ah may nevah get to see him befoah he passes away. If y'all let me say hello tah mah folks in Huntsville, Alabama, ah'll make yoah damned statement."

The general tapped his swagger stick on the palm of his hand. "Of course. We let all of our prisoners tell the American public how well they are treated."

"It's mah folks ah want to tell. Theah the ones who cayah about me the most. They raised me. Ah owe it to 'em. Especially mah daddy. He won't be around much longah."

The swagger stick tapped rapidly in his palm as the general looked up at the ceiling. He looked back down at Campbell. "We will write the statement. If you do not read it exactly, it will not be broadcast. Do you understand?"

"Yes, suh. Ah unduhstand that. They live in Huntsville, Alabama. If y'all write mah folks into yoah statement, ah'll read it. If y'all don't, then them gahds maht as well get it ovah with, 'cause ah won't say ah word."

The general hesitated a moment. He looked at Campbell's bruised and scabbed face, his swollen lips, his torn and filthy flight suit. He tapped the swagger stick into the palm of his hand. "I will arrange for tomorrow morning. You will get a full meal and be treated according to the Convention now that you decide to cooperate. We need the information you have not give to us. Your service number, date of birth and everything."

"Suh, ah mean no disrespect, but ah will not disclose the location of mah unit, nor the type of ayahcraft, nor mah tahget assahnments, noah anything else. If y'all want me to make a statement and say ah'm against the wah and that y'all are treatin' me well, ah'll do that. But ah will not disclose any military infoahmation, othah than mah name, rank, service numbah, and date of birth."

The general stood in deep thought.

Damn, maybe I made it look too easy. Christ, that can't be. What the hell do I have to do to convince this asshole? I'm not gonna kiss his ass. Yes I will if I can pull this off. That's stupid, Campbell. Get a grip. Square away. He stood silently, his face impassive, while the general considered his options. *Come on, you pompous bastard, go for it.*

After several long moments, the general looked him in the eyes and said, "You wait, Captain." He faced the doctor. "Clean him." Quickly, he turned and left the room.

Campbell sat on the bunk, his knees shaking uncontrollably. He was glad he hadn't carried his dog tags with him on this mission. *What if I gave something away while I was on those damn drugs? No, I must not have or they'd have shot me by now.* If they caught him in a lie, he knew he was dead. He smiled as he thought of his dog tags laying on top of his utility uniform in his footlocker. He didn't think pilots should have to carry dog tags anyway. *When the plane's down, they know who the pilot is. It's not like being a grunt. I was right this time. That's one for me.* A smile spread across his face. Campbell had no inkling how far along the Iraqis were in their ability to produce nuclear weapons but he wouldn't take a chance. Humiliating himself on worldwide television was a small price to pay if he could get his message to the Allies. *Bob will get things started. He'll remember. Goddamnit, Bob, you better remember.*

Campbell sat at the small table, across from the impeccably dressed Interviewer. The grey Formica of the table matched Campbell's mood. For twenty-four hours he'd had plenty of food, water and sleep. The cuts and scabs on his face had been washed, and though his body was sore and tender from the many beatings, it felt as if it was already beginning to heal.

He wondered how the war was going and hoped he wouldn't miss all of it before he escaped. He hung onto the thought of escape, though feebly. He looked into the smiling face of the interviewer. *Escape's my redemption.* He smiled. *This statement's only an interest payment.*

The cameras opposite the table began to roll, the whirring noises jarring his senses, adding to the trance-like feeling that possessed him. *This isn't really happening. It's a dream, a goddamned nightmare. I'll wake up in a minute to the sound of that damn bosun's whistle.* He tried to recall the beginning of this mission. The deck of the carrier loomed in his mind. He blanked it. He concentrated on his southern accent. Through his puffy right eye, he looked at the statement on the table in front of him. The typed words on the paper went in and out of focus. *There's so much to remember. Did I give them the right information? I sure as hell hope so. If I change anything that's printed on that paper, they won't let this tape get outside the country.*

The interviewer nodded and Campbell read:

"Mah name is James Campbell. Mah date of birth is January 31, 1960, and mah service numbah is 051-66-1165. Ah'm a captain in the United States Marine Coah. Since mah captuah by the peoples of Iraq, ah've had tahm tuh think ovah this unjust and unfayah wah aginst the peoples of Iraq. Ah have no desiah to continue mah role in such a wah.

"Ah'm bein' well treated by mah captors, and ah wont mah folks in Huntsville, Alabama to know that ah'm fine and hope to see them as soon as this heah wah against the people of Iraq is ovah and the innocent people have prevailed."

With his head still bowed, Campbell looked into the camera through puffy eyes, the lens blurry through his right eye. The cameraman stopped filming and Campbell was jerked from the chair. He offered little resistance. The drugs they had been

21

shooting into him depressed him and weakened his physical strength. What strength he had left, he would save for his mind.

CHAPTER 2

"They must have worked him over pretty good. Did you see the shiners and the dried blood? They couldn't even hide it from the T.V. cameras, for chrissake," said a young Marine second lieutenant as he pointed to a blank television screen, his blond hair barely discernable on his closely cropped head. He was young and tanned, like a commercial for a California lifeguard. His square jaw jutted indignantly at the screen, and his well-developed muscles strained at the confines of his uniform, adding to the image.

Major Robert Wyman sat across the large oak table from General Isaac Lewendoski. He cast a quick glance at the young lieutenant and rolled his dark green eyes to the ceiling. A staff of intelligence experts, representing every branch of the service, sat crowded into chairs closely packed around the table. The room was stuffy despite the sixty-degree temperature outside. The Saudi Arabian sun squeezed through the slits in the Venetian blinds in the old petroleum office building. A pesky, out-of-season fly buzzed noisily around and through the shafts of light.

Wyman's clean but wrinkled khaki uniform covered his six-foot frame loosely, casually. Small dark circles around his wide eyes gave testimony that he had not slept for quite some time. His forehead wrinkled beneath a lock of unkempt, rusty hair. It was longer than specified by Marine Corps regulations, but he felt little concern for that minor violation as he faced the Army general opposite his chair.

The general glanced about the room then turned to

Wyman. "How well do you know this man, Major?" His voice was gruff and raspy.

"Very well, sir. He's one of the best marines I've ever had the privilege to serve with. He's an ex-enlisted infantryman. Ex-Force Recon; ex-forward observer. Hell, he's done it all. After four years as an enlisted man, he went through college on one of the service programs, then O.C.S., then flight training. He's one of the best pilots in any man's air force, and he's as tough as they come."

Lewendoski gave him a sympathetic look. "It would appear he's been put through quite an ordeal, Major. Everyone has his limit."

"They might break anybody in the world but I don't think they broke him. He looks at life like a big game and he wants to play it his way or not at all." Wyman experienced a brief moment of anger at Lewendoski. *I know he didn't break. You may not know, but I do.*

The general leaned forward. "Then what's he trying to tell us, Major?"

"I'm not certain, Sir, but a few things crossed my mind as I was watching that tape."

"Get on with it, man." Lewendoski raised his voice and thumped the table impatiently with his hands.

"Well, as you know, Captain Campbell isn't from the south and he doesn't have a southern accent. Both of his parents were killed in a car accident when he was about ten years old. And his service number is nowhere near what he said it was on that Iraqi broadcast."

Lewendoski arched his eyebrows.

The young lieutenant held up a file folder. "Excuse me sir, but he didn't give us the right date of birth, either."

Lewendoski glanced at the lieutenant. "Thank you, Lieutenant." He looked back at Wyman. "Why the phoney accent? And why did he pick Huntsville, Alabama?"

24

Desert Fire

"I'm not sure, sir, but Jim and I were in Pensacola last year for some training. One weekend, we drove up to Huntsville to go through the rocket museum up there. Jim -- Captain Campbell -- likes to visit museums. And I have a lady friend there, so I joined him. Anyway, they had a missile on display that impressed him. I can't recall the name of it, but the thing that really impressed Jim was that missile's ability to carry a nuclear warhead. He kept saying over and over how amazing it was that such a small missile could deliver a nuclear warhead more than five hundred miles. That's the thing that stands out most in my mind about Huntsville." *Except for Clare.*

"Anything else happen in Huntsville, Major?"

Wyman smiled. "Well, sir, there was this brunette, but I'm not so sure she has much to do with his code."

General Lewendoski returned the smile. "Probably not, but let's have someone look her up. Do you know how to reach her?"

"Yessir. She was my date's sister."

"Jot down her address and phone number. I'm sure you marines carry that kind of tactical information around in your heads." Laughter made its way around the table.

The second lieutenant spoke up again. "Excuse me, General, but there's another question about the reason for his exaggerated southern accent."

Lewendoski looked at the young officer. "Lieutenant?"

"Well, sir, I suggest that there was no need for him to use that heavy accent when he was able to give us a specific location in the south. Since he gave us the location in the open, the accent might suggest another code, or at least another part of the same code."

"Or it may have been the cover he needed to claim a hometown in the south," offered a navy commander.

The marine lieutenant countered. "Or it may have had a dual use: code and cover. The accent was too heavy. He was over doing it."

Stoney Livingston

The general raised an eyebrow. He took his attention from the note Wyman was busily preparing and looked at the marine lieutenant. "What's your name, son?"

"Griswold, sir. Lieutenant Geoffrey Griswold."

"You're not Colonel Skip Griswold's son are you?"

"Yessir."

"I've heard of you. You've already got quite a reputation in intelligence."

Griswold looked down at a stack of papers on the table in front of him. "Thank you, sir."

Lewendoski nodded towards Wyman. "I want you to team up with Major Wyman here and together maybe the two of you can crack this code – if there is one. You won't have much time though. I don't want to keep the major from the flightline any longer than is necessary."

"Yessir!"

Wyman looked up from his unfinished note. "Sir. Begging the general's pardon, but I'm a carrier pilot, not an intelligence expert. I don't know the first thing about cracking a code."

Lewendoski smiled. "That's why I've assigned Lieutenant Griswold to assist you. I want him to pick your brain for a day or two. See what he can find out about Campbell from you. Then you can report back to your outfit."

"But, sir, I'm trained to fly fighter jets. I can tell the good lieutenant everything I know in five or six hours. The men in my squadron need me at the front. I…"

"That will be quite enough, Major. I need you to work on this code. You know the man better than anyone in the service." He paused. "You may actually find this a better way to serve your country."

"Yessir." Disappointment was clear in his voice. He wanted to be in the cockpit of his F-18 where the action was, not sitting behind a desk, shooting a pencil. He wanted to strike a blow for Jim against Iraq – with a bomb, not a piece of paper. *The*

26

sooner we win this thing, the sooner Jim's freed.

"This whole thing may be an exercise in futility." Lewendoski cast a quick glance at the blank tv screen. "We may be looking at nothing more than a beaten and drugged prisoner of war. Maybe we're trying to read something into all of this that just isn't there."

"There *is* a message somewhere in that statement, sir," said Wyman.

Lewendoski looked at Wyman and picked up the note. "Major, you and Lieutenant Griswold are dismissed from the meeting. I want you two to get started right away." He paused. "It's not all that bad, Major. I know you want back out there. That's understandable, but this takes precedence. See Major Wilson of my staff. You'll find him in this building – room 114. He'll set you up with quarters."

Wyman pushed his chair back and stood stiffly to attention. "Yes, sir." Lewendoski had a good reputation but Wyman didn't particularly care for army officers ordering marines around, even if he was a general. He was glad marines do not salute indoors unless under arms. He wasn't in the mood to salute anybody. He did an about face and left the room, Lieutenant Griswold on his heels.

Outside of the conference room, Wyman put his pisscutter on his head, cocked it over his right eye, and stepped out into the bright sun. He turned to Griswold. "You got a nickname, Griswold?"

Griswold snapped to attention and saluted smartly. "No, sir."

Wyman returned the smart salute with a sloppy one of his own. "Well, you got one now. And quit that damned salutin' every time I talk to you. Christ, if we're going to be together twenty-four hours a day until I report back to my unit, my arm'll fall off."

"Yessir!" Griswold saluted again, out of habit.

"I swear, if I see your hand above your shoulders again for

anything other than eatin' your chow or removing your cover, I'll break the damn thing off and beat you with the bloody stump. Do I make myself clear this time?"

"Yessir." His hand started upward but he stopped it at the waist.

Both men looked at each other intently for a moment. Wyman smiled first, then Griswold. Suddenly both men laughed.

"What nickname do I have now, sir?"

"Buzz. And quit calling me 'sir' as long as we're working this code thing together."

"'Buzz'?"

"Yeah. 'Buzz'."

"But why 'Buzz', sir?"

"Because your damned hair looks like it was cut with a buzzsaw. And you called me 'sir' again, damnit."

"What should I call you?"

"Bob. My name is Bob. How long have you been in the Corps?"

"Almost eighteen months, si. . Bob. Yeah. Almost eighteen months."

"Almost a whole-damn-eighteen-months." Wyman began a brisk walk on the neat sidewalk in front of the row of office buildings. He glanced at the vast expanse of desert to the west, then toward the nearby ocean only a half-mile from where he stood. The smell of the salt air reminded him of his carrier. A picture of Campbell's F-18 flashed through his mind. He shook his head and continued his brisk walk. *I've become a goddamn office poge, and I've even got a wet-nosed second lieutenant office-clerk-type shadow.*

"Where are you going, Si. . Bob? I mean where are *we* going? I mean, we should see Major Wilson and get your quarters lined up."

Wyman looked back over his shoulder at Buzz. "I feel a gut ache coming on." He looked back at the building, then to Buzz. "I want some chow before I get too sick to eat. I've got a feeling I'm gonna need my strength in the days ahead. We've got time for lunch. C'mon."

Buzz fell in behind, moving at the double to catch up, his starched khaki uniform swishing the air around him with each step.

Later that afternoon, Wyman stared blankly at a television screen as Buzz re-played the tape of Campbell's broadcast statement. His mind focused on the screen long enough for Campbell's battered image to re-plant itself in his brain. He smashed the small coffee table with his fist. "Damn!"

Buzz snapped around. "What's wrong?"

Wyman composed himself. "Nothing." He glanced at the screen. "Bullshit. There's what's wrong." He pointed at the screen.

Buzz shut off the VCR. The screen bubbled with white and grey specks in a moving sea of electrons. He moved from his position on the floor in front of the TV set to a chair next to the small sofa where Wyman sat. Buzz sank into the low, overstuffed chair, leaned back and stretched his legs. "I know you want to get back to the war, but you can probably do more for him by telling me everything you can think of about the guy." He raised his arms over his head and squeezed his hands together. "We finished chow more than two hours ago. I know it's tough, but we've gotta get something done."

Some of the tenseness left Wyman's jaw muscles. "Yeah, I guess you're right. It's just kind of hard for me to believe this whole thing. You'd have to know Jim to understand that. None of it's real for me yet." He rubbed his hands together. "Let's get started. What do you want to know?"

"Everything you know about the man."

"That'll take volumes. We've known each other for more than three years."

Buzz pulled a small tape recorder from his briefcase and

set it on the coffee table. "I've got plenty of tape. Start with the day you met him."

Wyman looked around the room. "I wish to hell we had a bottle of bourbon. Can't figure out why they'd put marines in a country where it's a sin to drink booze. Seems to be an irony in there somewhere."

"Maybe we can find a bottle somewhere."

Wyman shook his head. "I don't want to be the one to cause an international uproar."

"I understand you weren't always so concerned about diplomacy."

Wyman looked at Buzz. "What are you talking about?"

Buzz shrugged. "I did my homework. That's what I'm supposed to do. A couple of years ago, I understand you and Jim Campbell caused a bit of an international incident."

"You mean that little deal down in Mexico?"

"There wasn't much on it officially but I talked to Colonel Stills. He filled in between the lines," said Buzz.

"How much did he fill in?"

"Everything he knew," answered Buzz.

"Everything?"

Buzz smiled. "I told him it was for intelligence purposes only. I don't have any intention of turning over old dirt for disciplinary reasons."

"That guy had it coming."

"He was the mayor of the town."

"He was a crook. He had me arrested for no reason other than to shake me down."

"Who's idea was it to lock him and his police department in their own jail after Campbell busted you out?"

Wyman thought a moment, his eyes searching the ceiling. He looked at Buzz and grinned. "I'd like to say it was mine – but I gotta admit – Jim came up with the idea. Made me madder'n hell I didn't think of it first. But stripping 'em all to their shorts, that was my idea."

Both men laughed loudly.

Wyman thought about that night fondly. His laughter faded to a warm smile. "Yeah, when Jim came bustin' into that place with that M-16 in one hand and a grenade in the other, I thought I was gonna split a gut. He was all painted up in camouflage paint, looking like a grunt, and talking Mexican faster'n a Puerto Rican. The guy at the desk outside my cell didn't know whether to shit or go blind. Jim had him in my cell before he could make up his mind, and we were home free."

Buzz grinned a wide grin. "So why didn't you just leave the place and get back across the border?"

"Jim thought it would be a good idea to have a little insurance."

"Is that why he called in the whole police department and the mayor?"

"He found the phone numbers in a desk drawer and, as good as he speaks Spanish, it was a cinch. Those guys came walking in the door, thinking they were gonna have first dibs on three cars stolen up in Texas."

Buzz's laughter erupted into the room. "I wish I could have seen the looks on their faces."

Wyman clicked his tongue against the roof of his mouth. "I'm tellin' ya, Buzz, it was worth a million bucks. Then, to add insult to injury, we drove the mayor's car across the border and dropped it off at the police station on our side. Took 'em two days to find a serial number that the mayor's boys forgot to grind off, but they found one. Seems like the honorable mayor was driving a stolen American car."

"I understand that same honorable mayor decided not to press for extradition."

Wyman raised an eyebrow. "That would have been a bit embarrassing, don't you think?"

"What else can you tell me about Jim Campbell? He was

picked for intelligence training just before he went to flight school. Seems he flunked out on the entrance tests. From what I can see of his background that appears inconsistent as hell with his abilities."

Wyman laughed loudly. "Oh no, Buzz, old man. It's *consistent* as hell with his abilities. He had his mind made up he was going to be a fighter pilot. He deliberately flunked those tests."

"Deliberately?"

Wyman nodded.

"How can you be so sure? This was before you ever met him."

"I hate to bust the bubbles of all the experts who think they know so damn much, but Jim Campbell would have made the best intelligence officer in the Marine Corps – *if* he wanted to be – but he didn't. So, he did the next best thing – he flunked the entrance exams. That way, he got to go to flight school, and the experts were satisfied he didn't have the moxy to be in intelligence."

"I knew there was something wrong with the scores but I figured maybe a woman problem. How can you be so sure it wasn't?" asked Buzz.

Wyman looked at Buzz intently. He studied the blond eyelashes of the younger man, then his jaw, then his haircut, mouth, chin, eyes. *Do I trust this kid or not? That's the damn question.* He whispered. "Buzz, I want to help Jim, but if the brass found out, they'd know he deliberately flunked that test and, more importantly, I'd be breaking my word to Jim. The Corps doesn't know and Jim doesn't want them to find out. He's afraid they'll try to make some damn kind of secret weapon out of him."

Buzz leaned closer. "What the hell are you talking about? What is it, Bob?"

Wyman slouched back in the sofa. "Jim is one of those rare people who can recite a book, cover-to-cover, having only read the damn thing once. He's got a photographic memory."

The sun was low on the horizon. Wyman closed the blinds on the window to shut out the intense light from the west. Buzz sat next to his tape recorder, tapping a pencil between two perfect rows of teeth.

"You want some chow?" asked Buzz.

"I'm not really very damn hungry. How 'bout you?"

Buzz smiled broadly. "Hell, if the story stays as good as it's been so far, I won't take the time out to eat for at least a week yet."

"It's true. Every damn word."

"Jim sounds like an egg-head, you know, the brainy type with the horned rim glasses – skinny little guy – who was champion of the chess team."

"He's not all that big – five-foot-ten – but he's a hell of an athlete. By the way, he won't play chess. He did it in high school for awhile. Not even the champion of the chess club down in Las Cruces could beat him. I'm telling you, he's something else!

"One time we were driving west on Interstate Ten, just east of Mobile. We stopped to help a trucker with a flat steering tire. The driver asked us to stop at the truck stop on the east end of town and ask them to send a service truck with a new tire. When we pulled into that truck stop, the guy in the tire shop asked us what size tire the trucker needed.

"Hell, Jim and I thought all those eighteen-wheelers used the same size tire – big. Anyway, Jim closed his eyes real hard and concentrated on a mental picture of the flat tire. Next thing I knew, he said, 'Is 11X24.5 a tire size?'

"Well, that ol' boy at the truck stop just looked at Jim like he was crazy and said, 'No shit, Sherlock. Where'd you come up with it? Are you guessin' or are you rememberin'?'

"Jim kept his eyes closed and said, 'I'm reading it, goddamnit. I don't know anything about truck tire sizes. How the

33

hell else would I know it if I couldn't read it?'"

Buzz fell off his chair. Tears of laughter rolled down his face. He gasped for breath. "I've gotta...meet...this guy."

The smile faded from Wyman's face. "You will, Buzz. You will. I know you will, goddamnit. He's gonna come out of this."

The morning of their second day together, right after morning chow, Buzz and Wyman returned to the latter's room. Wyman continued his story-telling session until almost noon, Buzz taking notes all the time. After noon chow, they came straightaway back to the room and Buzz turned on the VCR.

"You ready, Bob?"

He nodded.

Buzz started the tape. "I'm going to run it without sound."

Wyman's jaw tightened again as he saw the battered face for the umpteenth time. He felt his friend's pain as Campbell blinked his eyes and fidgeted with his hands on the grey Formica tabletop. *Those bastards! What the hell have they done to him?*

The silently moving lips and blinking eyes appeared absurd – except that Wyman could hear the words in his mind. *What are you trying to tell us, old friend? What are you trying to tell us?*

The picture froze. Wyman looked at Buzz. An expression of discovery covered the young lieutenant's face. His eyes were wide and his mouth hung limply open.

"What the hell is it?" asked Wyman.

Buzz rewound the tape to the beginning. He rubbed his hands together in anticipation. "He *is* telling us something."

"No shit. How long did you say you went to this intelligence school?"

"Not with his voice – with his body – with his eyes. Can you read Morse Code?"

Wyman arched an eyebrow. "Before you got out of diapers."

"Watch." Buzz moved the tape forward in slow motion, his

pen and pad in his lap. He pointed to the screen. "Look. It starts here. Let me get it. See. He blinks both eyes several times. 'E D R'. Then he blinks his right eye once. I don't know what that means. Then he blinks both eyes and sends 'O T M'. Then he blinks his left eye once." Buzz froze the tape and looked at Wyman. "What do you suppose that means?"

"Hell, I don't know. Run that back and let me look at it again. Run it regular speed and let me see if I can pick up the Morse Code."

Buzz rewound the tape and ran it at normal speed to the part where Campbell spelled out 'O T M'. He froze it there.

Wyman looked at Buzz and said, "I'll be goddamned. I think you're right. He sent 'E D R' and 'O T M'. Maybe that blinking of a single eye was to throw the Iraqis off, or maybe he just had to blink his eye for real."

"Maybe, but I don't think so. Let's look at a little more." He started up the tape and let it roll silently to its end. When it was over, he turned to Wyman. "Did you notice anything?"

"Yeah. I noticed he didn't do anymore code with his eyes."

"Maybe. Maybe not," said Buzz.

"What the hell are you talking about?"

"I didn't pick up on any *Morse Code*, but he may have been sending a *different* kind of code."

Wyman leaned closer to Buzz. *For a second lieutenant, this guy is pretty damn good.* "What different kind of code?"

Buzz shook his head. "I don't know."

"Great." *Then again...*

"But maybe it's connected to the first two sets of letters. He blinks one eye once – maybe three or four times, then he blinks the other several times. There's a pattern but I can't figure it out yet."

"Maybe you're reading too much into it. Maybe all he felt he could get to us safely were those two sets of letters and the rest is just natural blinking, or maybe to throw them off. I mean, after all, take a look at what they did to him. I imagine you'd be doing a little blinking yourself if those damn ragheads worked you over like they obviously did him."

Buzz scratched on a piece of paper.

"How long ago was it we checked the info pool?" asked Wyman.

Buzz glanced at his watch. "Ten minutes."

Wyman picked up the phone. "I'm going to try it again."

"They probably would have notified us if anybody had a substantial clue." Buzz continued to scribble.

Wyman put the receiver back in its cradle. "Damnit, Buzz, I know Jim didn't send a code this complicated. How could he send something that our experts can't figure out? I know the man. It would be something simple."

Buzz said, "That's it!" His voice had a high pitch to it.

Wyman looked sharply at him and moved to the edge of the sofa. "You come up with something?"

"I don't know for sure, but what you said makes sense. What if, in order to break this code, we had to know something or someone else? You know, like the pirate maps and stuff we used to draw as kids: you go here first, then there, then finally, 'X marks the spot?'"

"That's a little cloudy to me, old man. What the hell are you talking about?"

"Think about it. What definite clues has he given us?"

"Huntsville, Alabama. Folks who are dead. A phony service number and date of birth. And a southern accent that would put Scarlet O'Hara to shame."

"And six letters, in groups of three each, in Morse Code."

"And fingers tapping and fidgeting when he was talking."

"I think that was a cover. I can't pick a code out of it yet anyway," said Buzz.

Wyman felt his excitement fade, like a golf ball as it leaves the tee and disappears into the fairway. "Hell, we already knew what we saw. We just didn't know what it meant. That's nothing new. Where's the breakthrough?"

"Look at this." Buzz pointed to a piece of paper. "Ignore the scratch marks and doodles. See what happens when we regroup the letters? We get 'tom' and 'red'."

"So?"

Buzz looked disappointed. "I was hoping you knew someone with those names."

"Hell, I probably know a hundred people named Tom, and at least a dozen called Red. What the hell is that supposed..." Wyman looked directly into Buzz's eyes. A frown crossed his face.

"Something wrong, Bob?"

"Mutt and Jeff."

"Mutt and Jeff?" Repeated Buzz.

"Mutt and Jeff. Two guys in our wing. They're the best of friends. They're a team. Their real names are Thomas Posner and Rudolph Redd."

"Rudolph Redd?"

Wyman shrugged. "I didn't name him, goddamnit."

"What about them?"

"They're both damn good pilots. Jeff is almost as good as I am." Wyman smiled.

"Jeff?"

"Redd. He's Jeff. He's short. Mutt's got about a foot on him. Mutt is Tom."

"I figured that last part out. How can Mutt – Posner – Tom – whatever his name is, fly? Isn't he too tall?"

Wyman shook his head. "He just made it."

"Well, it's a start. Let's get copies of their service record books faxed to us and see if we can come up with anything. Can you think of any other pairs of 'tom' and 'red'?"

Wyman shook his head. "I'll get on the horn. We should have copies of those service record books here in less than an hour."

It was almost daylight when they fell asleep. Each had gone through the record books of Posner and Redd at least ten times apiece without a single clue as to how either of the two men could be connected to the code.

Shortly after eight in the morning, the phone rang. Wyman looked for Buzz and found him asleep on the floor. He smacked his lips and ran his tongue around the inside of his mouth, then picked up the phone. "Major Wyman."

A gruff voice greeted him. "Major, this is General Lewendoski."

"Good morning, Sir." *Maybe they've come up with something.* He felt a surge of anticipation.

"How are you and Lieutenant Griswold doing? Come up with anything yet?"

"No, sir, not yet." The anticipation disappeared into a vacuum. "Has anybody else figured this thing out?"

"Afraid not. I just wanted you to know that you'll be cleared to return to your normal duty station in twenty-four hours. By then, Lieutenant Griswold should have everything he needs to crack the code, *if* there is one."

"Sir. There *is* a code there. I *know* the man."

"That's why I kept you here, major. You've got twenty-four more hours to prove me right. If there's a code, find the damn thing."

"Yessir."

The phone went dead. Wyman looked at Buzz's face, innocent in sleep, showing no wrinkles of time and worry. *You don't know it yet, Buzz, old boy, but we're gonna find out what Jim was saying. And we're gonna do it before tomorrow morning at this time.*

CHAPTER 3

It was the midnight of his televised statement. Campbell stared at the guard's wrist, angry at what he saw. *It's been missing since I first regained consciousness at the mercy of Bozo and Howdy Doody. I thought one of those two clowns got it. This guy must have connections.* The watch on the guard's wrist was one of Jim Campbell's prized possessions. His grandfather had given it to him as a high school graduation present. *That seems like a hundred years ago.*

There were only four boys and three girls in the high school graduation class from the Mescalero Reservation High School in 1977. The commencement exercises took place on a hot May evening, in a natural amphitheater, in a grove of pine trees taller than most of the skyscrapers in the state of New Mexico.

George Chitla, his full-blooded Apache maternal grandfather, and Maria, his grandmother, sat silently in the crowd of parents, families, and friends. Though they didn't speak, young Jim Campbell felt the warmth of their pride cover him like a blanket of July sunshine.

It had been difficult for Jim after his parents died in the car crash but, with his grandparents help and support, he had done well in school, both in athletics and academics. His grandfather urged him to overload himself in high school and Jim had almost done just that, but he managed to make it without succumbing to the temptation to quit school and find a job off the reservation.

In the middle of his senior year he had gone with his grandparents to visit relatives in Sante Fe. At the market in the town square, on the sidewalk of the oldest government building still in use by a government agency, he had seen the watch. It was the band more than the watch he wanted. It was a simple band of Mexican silver, with two turquoise stones mounted on each side of the watch on a black background.

He had picked up the watchband and studied it with great care. And after asking the Navajo woman the price, he had quickly returned it its proper place on the table. His Grandfather appeared not to notice.

When the graduation ceremony had ended, Jim had walked stiffly up to his grandparents. He had faced his grandfather awkwardly and held out his diploma. "This is for all of us, Grandfather, but it is especially for you, because without you to push me when I needed pushing, I wouldn't have it."

His grandfather accepted the diploma. "I will keep it safe for you until you need it." He turned to his wife and put his hand inside her purse. He withdrew a small felt box from inside and held it out to Jim. "And this is for you. I hope you wear it proudly and it serves you well. It contains the technical knowledge of your father's culture and the artistic knowledge of our Navajo brothers to the north. It is like you, the best of both."

Jim opened the box and saw the watch. It was the same one he had seen in Santa Fe. His grandfather had not seemed to notice Jim looking at the watch at the time but little escaped the old man's attention, and he had somehow managed to get it for his grandson. Jim tried to stand still and shake his grandfather's hand and thank him like a man, but he couldn't. He fell into the older man's arms and cried. "It's beautiful, Grandfather. But it was so expensive. I can't..."

"Don't say anymore, Jim. Your grandmother and I want you to have this watch and band. It makes us happier than it makes you. I guess that may mean we are selfish, but sometimes people are that way."

Jim had put the watch on his wrist, and rarely had it left his touch in the years that followed.

The guard with his watch came on duty every night at midnight, and always he asked Campbell, "Hey, Flyboy. Guess what time?"

Campbell held his composure with great difficulty and smiled sweetly every night. "Got no ahdea, theah, Ahab. Whah don't y'all tell me?"

The guard's crooked and yellow teeth made Campbell want to gag as he watched the thin lips curl into a sneer. "Look like midnight, Flyboy."

After the broadcast, Campbell played the defeated and disillusioned soldier. He praised Allah and the Iraqi cause, and he apologized profusely to his guards for the wrongful destruction being wrought upon their country. His hope of gaining the trust of his captors diminished by the hour. They watched him vigilantly whenever he was escorted from his room. Doctor Kildare visited him every day in the late afternoon, and carried the dreaded needle and syringe.

I already made the televised statement. They don't need to drug me in order to achieve that end. What the hell else are they looking for? Whatever it was, Campbell felt certain he wasn't giving it to them.

The third afternoon following his televised statement, Campbell heard a loud commotion in the hall outside his room. He jumped from his bunk and moved quickly to the door to get a better view of what was going on. His eyes grew wide at the sight of a U.S. Air Force major, in his flight suit, being pushed down the hall, his hands tied behind him, fighting his captors every step of the way.

A young Iraqi soldier – Campbell had nicknamed him "Dopey" for his sleepy look – stood just outside the room. Campbell tapped the door. Dopey turned and looked stupidly at him.

"Hey, Dopey. I gotta pee."

"You wait."

Campbell shook his head. "Can't wait. It's an emergency. C'mon, man. I gotta go!"

Reluctantly, Dopey opened the door. Campbell stepped into the hallway. The Air Force major was only fifteen feet away, showing his contempt for his two guards by scowling and swearing at them.

"Keep the faith, Major." Campbell shot him a "V" sign by holding up the first two fingers of his right hand.

The major spun to face him. "Captain Campbell?"

"Small world, huh?"

"No talk!" One of the guards pulled the major roughly by his tied hands and spun him into the wall.

"Hey, raghead, lighten up, y'all heah?" shouted Campbell.

At the threatening sound of Campbell's voice, the two guards pointed their rifles at his chest. He stared into their faces. "*Mah* hands ahn't tied, asshole." He addressed the man who had thrown the major into the wall. "Whah don't y'all throw *me* around?"

The man took a step in his direction, his rifle centered on Campbell's breastbone. Campbell held his ground, nostrils flaring.

"It isn't worth it, Campbell." The major had regained his feet. Blood from his nose ran over his upper lip and dropped to the floor.

The other guard faced the major. "No talk!"

"Okay. It's okay. No talk," said the major.

The guard confronting Campbell stared into his face. The two men had locked eyes and neither would look away. The guard moved towards him, ready to swing the butt of his rifle.

Dopey jumped in front of Campbell and chattered rapidly. The major's guard said something in reply. Dopey pointed to the rank on his uniform and the guard relaxed and moved back to the major with a parting glance at Campbell. They shoved the major down the hall and out of sight around a corner.

"Keep in touch, you heah?" shouted Campbell as the major disappeared.

Dopey tapped him on the shoulder. "No talk."

Campbell turned and looked at him in disgust. "Piss on you, Dopey."

"Yeah. Go piss. Quick."

Campbell shook his head and walked slowly to the bathroom, hoping he could pee when he got there.

To keep in shape, Campbell did push-ups, sit-ups and stationary double-time three times a day. At first, his guards eyed him suspiciously, but he told them all he planned to escape and he wanted to be in shape for the big day, and they laughed. *They probably think the drugs have made me lose it. Maybe they have.*

Campbell's daily diet of rice returned immediately after his televised statement. Not only was he on a rice diet, but there was less rice on his plate than there had been before. He grew weaker daily despite his physical regimen.

He longed to see the sun again but his captors denied him his wish. Except for the marks he made on the wall next to his bunk to mark the passage of days, he knew nothing of time. The lights never went out inside the building, including the one in his room. Sleeping with the light on was difficult at first but he grew used to it by the third day and could fall asleep in a matter of seconds by telling himself it was rack time.

He played mental games with the officers who came to his room to question him every afternoon. He had dropped the southern accent on the second day after his statement. It had served its purpose. Now, if only Bob could understand what he had said...

The interrogator on this day reminded him of an old friend from Boston. He put on his best Boston accent. When the officer left the room, Doctor Kildare, who was always present at the sessions, gave Campbell another dose of whatever it was he carried in his syringe that day.

Campbell knew the drugs were not all the same. Some, he was certain, were sodium Pentothal. He could only guess at the others. *Cocaine? LSD? Heroin? Hell, who knows?*

Late in the afternoon of the day he saw the Air Force major, a tall captain with a thick mustache entered Campbell's room. Campbell sat on the floor and continued his sit-up routine as the captain stood over him. "Have a seat, Captain. I'll be with you in a second."

"I must say, you are a cool one." The captain's English was grammatically perfect, but his accent was thick.

"...ninety-nine, one hundred." Campbell got to his feet slowly. "What can I do for you, Captain?"

"No, Captain Campbell, it is what I can do for you that is important."

Campbell looked at him, a grin on his face. "You gonna give me a machinegun and the keys to the front door?"

The Iraqi captain smiled weakly. "My name is Abdul Ishtoul. I am your counsel."

"Yeah? Well, let me give *you* a little counsel. Talk your boss into givin' up while he still has a chance and you'll save us both a lot of trouble. Nice to meet you there, Abdul, baby." Campbell sat on the edge of his bunk and patted the other end of the mattress. "Have a seat. Relax. Don't be afraid of my rank. I'm here to help you, Abdul, old man."

Abdul sat on the other end of the bunk. "Captain Campbell, I'm afraid you don't understand the seriousness of what I'm telling you."

Campbell ignored his statement. "Hell you haven't told me anything yet. By the way, where'd you learn to speak English? It wasn't in the States. You know, your grammar and lexicon are excellent, but you really ought to work on that accent. Sounds like you're trying to speak two languages at the same time when you talk."

"Captain, how I pronounce my words will be of little consequence to you if you are found guilty of war crimes."

The smile left Campbell's face. He looked hard into the Iraqi captain's face. "War crimes? What war crimes? Are you crazy?"

"You have been charged with war crimes. If you are found guilty, you will be shot. Now, may I have your attention?"

"May you have my attention? May you have my goddamned attention? Sure. You got it. That was a hell of an opening line there, Abdul. When do we go to this kangaroo court?"

"Soon."

"Soon? What the hell kind of answer is that? C'mon, I gotta know within a little smaller bracket than that. I need to know when to leave this dump. I don't really care for the accommodations here anyway."

"This is a very serious matter, Captain Campbell."

"No shit. Who says I'm not being serious?"

Abdul stared blankly at the window in the door. "I think the trial will start in about four or five days."

Campbell felt his heart fall to his stomach. He smiled. "How long does the trial for a war criminal last?"

"Probably one day." Abdul continued to stare at the door.

Campbell clicked his tongue against the roof of his mouth. "Too bad justice can't be carried out that quickly in the States. I guess too many attorneys would starve to death." He paused. "How long after my *fair trial* before they shoot me?"

"The next day."

Campbell sighed. "Do they give the condemned man a last cigarette?"

Abdul nodded.

Campbell clapped his hands together. "Think they might let me request my own brand ahead of time? I don't like those damned filter cigarettes you ragheads smoke." He looked at the ceiling as he struggled to hide his despair. "I've been telling ol' Dopey out there I'm dying for a smoke. Guess I will, huh?"

A long moment of silence passed between them. Abdul spoke first. "It doesn't have to be that way. Tell them what they want to know and confess to your crimes and perhaps the court will show mercy."

"I don't want the mercy of a bunch of wimpy ragheads who couldn't fight their way out of a wet paper bag." He looked down at his torn and stained flight suit. "I was gonna have to throw this thing out anyway." He looked at Abdul. "So, what d'ya think, counsel? Should we plead temporary insanity?"

Abdul stood. "Perhaps in your case that plea would work. What is so important to the outcome of the war that you would remain silent and die, rather than tell what little you know and live?"

Campbell stared defiantly at him. "It doesn't have a damn thing to do with the war, or what I know or don't know. It has to do with assholes like you pushing people around. Well, counsel, I don't like being pushed around. I push back. Even if it kills me, I push back. If I fail, the next guy might not. One day, all the Saddam Husseins will be pushin' up daisies in unmarked graves, because they pushed one time too many."

"Eloquent, Captain. Very eloquent."

"It wasn't meant to be. Sorry if it went over your head."

Abdul took a step toward the door, stopped and turned around. "There will be no more drugs for a while unless you attempt to create a disruption at this facility."

"What's the special occasion?"

"We want you cognizant your last days on earth to contemplate your death."

"Fuck you, Counsel."

"And if you are not drugged, perhaps you will be able to give the other prisoner moral support as he undergoes interrogation. As you know, it can be quite an experience."

A picture of an Iraqi soldier kicking the American major in the groin, then smashing his face with leaded gloves flashed though Campbell's mind. He felt the pain. His stomach turned. He wanted to kill them all. If only he could reach a weapon. "Remind me to look you up after we win this war, Counsel."

"Good day, Captain." Abdul turned and left the room.

The major's screams pierced the fog in Campbell's brain. He sat up in his bed and looked at the guard through the window. *The one with my watch. It must be past midnight.* Again the ear-piercing scream shattered the stillness. Campbell stood and walked to the door.

The guard turned and smiled his crooked yellow smile. "Hey, Flyboy, guess what time?"

"Fuck you, Ahab."

"Look like midnight, Flyboy."

Campbell glared at him. *I wonder if the dumbshit can even tell time?* "I'm gettin' tired of that joke, Ahab. And I'm gettin' tired of all the noise. Tell our neighbors to keep it down or I'm gonna file a complaint."

Ahab put his face to the glass. "What you say? Too muchy noise. Talk loud."

"I said your mother was a two-bit whore."

Ahab smiled. "No understand."

Campbell waved him off and returned to his bunk. He sat on the edge of it and listened as the major's screams grew weaker. Campbell bit his lip and held his breath, his body trembling with hopeless rage as he pictured the scene in the interrogation room. *I could try to take out Ahab-the-Arab. Then what? Get me and the major both killed?* Another scream pierced the air. *At this point maybe he wouldn't give a damn.*

Dopey opened the door to Campbell's room and let in the

soldier carrying a plate of food. "Chow time," said the soldier evenly. He set the tray on the floor and left the room.

Campbell said nothing as he sat up in his bunk. He was tired. The cries of the major had kept him awake late. Campbell stood and completed his morning calisthenics. He was breathing heavily when he finished. He contemplated the food on the floor. *I hate this stuff, what little there is of it, but I've gotta keep up my strength.* The bowl of rice looked bland and unappetizing as it stared up at him from the center of the plate. *I can make it, one meal at a time. When I get back to the States, I'm gonna eat a whole damn steer.* He picked up a portion of rice between his thumb and index finger and stuffed it into his mouth, chewing twice before swallowing. He was on his fourth bite when he saw a bright flash and felt his body growing lighter.

Drugs! They've drugged my damn chow! He floated in the air and looked down at his body laying on the concrete floor, curled up in the fetal position. *Shit! Am I dead? What the hell is going on?*

He was no longer in the building. He was high in the air somewhere, somewhere he'd never been before, higher than he'd ever flown in any airplane. *I've gotta be dead. There can't be enough oxygen up here to support life.*

He was above the stratosphere and yet there were clouds. From a puffy white cloud, a form emerged. It was the form of a man, and yet it wasn't. Campbell couldn't identify it.

"Why have you come to me, infidel?" said the form.

"I didn't come to you. Who are you anyway?"

"I am many things to many people, but in your language, you call me God."

"God? Which god?"

"God."

"There are many gods if there is such a thing as a god. There is the god of the earth. The god of sun. The god of rain. Which one are you?"

Desert Fire

"You try my patience, James J. Campbell."

"James J. Campbell? That's a might formal, don't you think?"

"Enough. Why did you come to me?"

"We've already been through that."

"You are insolent, even in death, James J. Campbell."

"I'm dead?"

The form nodded, or at least it appeared to nod. Since he couldn't really focus on it, Campbell couldn't see the nod, but he knew he had been answered in the affirmative.

"Do dead people get any last requests?"

Another unseen nod.

"I want to go back to Iraq for a minute and square a few people away. Can I do that?"

"Are you certain this is what you want to do?"

"I've never been more certain of anything."

"It is done."

Campbell felt himself sinking. He passed through a thick layer of brightly colored clouds but, when he was below them, they were no longer there. A vast emptiness lay below. He was back in the weapons plant. The ground was cold. But he wasn't on the ground. He crashed into his prone body.

"Well, Captain, did you enjoy your trip?"

Campbell knew the voice. Where had he heard it before? He opened his eyes and watched the room spin about him. He reached out to grab something solid but his arms were tied to the edges of the bed. *Where the hell am I?* He looked into the smiling face of Abdul. "Why don't you go fuck a camel?"

The corner of Abdul's mouth twitched. "You are going to die today, Captain. I will allow you your fun."

"Today? What the hell happened to the trial?"

"We held the trial. I'm afraid the effects of the drug lasted longer than we had anticipated. You were no help at all in your own defense."

Stoney Livingston

"You're crazy."

"As you wish, Captain." He paused until a slow smile had worked its way across his face. "But it doesn't really matter now, does it?" He glanced at his watch. "You have only a matter of minutes left before you face the firing squad."

Campbell's heartbeat quickened. He continued a stoic look at Abdul. "I don't believe you."

Abdul clucked. "My good captain, you are about to become a true believer." He snapped his fingers and two guards quickly entered the room. Abdul spoke to them brusquely.

The two untied Campbell's hands from the bed and bound them behind his back. They stood him up and pushed him out the door of the room and into a strange hallway. They walked him between them as they made their way down the corridors. The lead man stopped and opened a door. The early morning sun had a grey tinge to it, dampening its affect on Campbell's unaccustomed   eyes.

They pushed him into a courtyard and stood him against a concrete wall. Campbell drew the smell of unfiltered air deeply into his lungs, wanting to get as much of it as he could before he left this place. He cast a slow glance about him. Only thirty feet to his right stood several vending machines. *It doesn't happen this way in the movies. Who the hell ever heard of vending machines as the only impartial witnesses at an execution?*

Through a gate to his left, seven soldiers armed with rifles marched into the courtyard and halted, the middle of their ranks centered on him. An officer stood between Campbell and the row of men. The two guards left him and re-entered the building. Campbell was alone with his assassins.

The row of soldiers faced sloppily to their right at the command of the officer and stood at attention. The officer faced Campbell and stood silent and rigid. Campbell stood as straight and as tall as he could, chin in, chest out. *Fuck you all.* His body trembled almost uncontrollably, partially a reaction to the drugs, but mostly the result of raw fear. *Don't let 'em see it, Campbell. Don't give 'em the satisfaction. They're going to kill you anyway. There's nothing you can do.*

The door next to the vending machines opened and Abdul, accompanied by the general with his swagger stick stepped into the courtyard. Both men approached Campbell slowly, deliberately. The general carried a large black handkerchief. The two stopped three feet in front of him.

"Captain Campbell, we offer you one last chance to save your life. Have you anything you wish to say?" said Abdul.

Campbell fought to retain control. He wanted to beg for his life. He had too many things yet to do before he died. "Yeah. Where's my cigarette?"

Abdul's face fell. He fished in his pocket and withdrew a pack of smokes. He withdrew one and put it to Campbell's lips. Campbell turned his head. "I told you I don't like those damn things. If I can't have an American cigarette, then I guess I'll have to do without. At this point I can afford to be choosey. Let's get this over with."

Campbell saw what he thought was a look of genuine sorrow in Abdul's eyes. *Don't delude yourself, Campbell. It doesn't matter anyway now.*

The general stepped forward and put the blindfold to Campbell's eyes. "What's the matter, General? Can't your boys look me in the eye when they pull the trigger?

The general jerked the blindfold away and stepped back. He turned to Abdul and spoke briefly, then moved to the end of the firing squad. Abdul looked into Campbell's face. "Please, Captain, I have done everything I can do. Don't be foolish. Tell them what they want to hear."

"I can't stand at attention much longer, Abdul, old man. Why don't you just back outa the way and let these shitheads do their job? Unless of course you want to join me?"

Silently, Abdul took a position next to the general. The

officer in charge of the firing squad took his position at Campbell's far right, at the end of the row. His voice was harsh and strong as it broke the stillness of the morning air in English. Campbell knew the English was for his benefit, designed to instill more fear. "Take position!" The rifle butts went into shoulders. "Ready!" Nothing moved. "Aim!" Campbell saw the squinted eyes of the individual soldiers as their fingers tightened on the triggers. Campbell tensed for the impact of the slugs. "Fire!" The echo of the officer's voice was drowned by the sharp crack of seven rifles.

Campbell's body lurched forward a fraction of an inch to meet the projectiles. He almost fell on his face. *Jesus! They all missed!* He regained his composure and stood as straight and tall as his shaky legs and knotted stomach would allow. His heart beat wildly in his temples. *Oh no! Goddamn. Don't lose it now. I can't stand it much longer. I can't go through it again.* The row of soldiers appeared wavy. *I'm passing out. Oh shit. I've gotta do something.* He looked over at Abdul and the general. "You guys can't shoot worth a shit." A greyness crawled into his vision. He fought it off, but only momentarily. Blackness engulfed him.

He was in his bunk. The grey concrete wall stared at him unemotionally. The marks were there. Nothing had changed. *How many days have gone by?*

"Congratulations, Captain."

Campbell turned his head away from the wall and looked into the face of Abdul. He felt his adrenaline building. He said nothing. Nothing seemed appropriate. The enemy had seen him give in to fear – fear induced by them.

"The last man we tried that experiment on died of a heart attack, a combination of the drugs, and a fear deeper than most of us ever know. Consider yourself privileged."

Campbell felt the rage creep up his body. He fought his impulse to grab Abdul by the throat. *Be cool. They can't win after this. Don't give 'em the game.* "How much time has passed since

I first ate that drugged rice?"

Abdul glanced at his watch. "Almost two hours."

Two hours! It had to be a week. "Give it to me straight for once. Quit bullshittin' around. You think I won't find a calendar when I bust outa here or something?"

"I'm telling you the truth this time. It was only two hours." Abdul's voice carried a note of respect.

"How's the other prisoner?"

Abdul shook his head. "Not well. He is not as strong as you. He grows weaker by the day."

"Why don't you lay off him? You'll all be tried in a real court for war crimes if you don't," said Campbell, the harshness gone from his voice.

Abdul shrugged. "It is not for me to say. I am a Captain, it is true, but I am a lawyer, not a soldier. These things are out of my control."

Campbell sat up, the effort causing him dizziness. His hands were free. He used one of them to steady himself. Abdul held him by the shoulders. "You should lay down for several hours yet."

Campbell focused his eyes then looked at Abdul. "I'm gettin' outa here, Abdul, old man. You do realize that, don't you?" He fell back onto his bunk and went to sleep.

Two days later, Campbell could no longer contain himself. The major was still alive but Campbell wouldn't give odds on how much longer he would last at the rate he was being tortured. The Iraqis had moved him closer. Campbell wondered why. *It's probably because his screams are too weak to be heard by me from the other interrogation room.* He planned to get his watch back, take the major, make an escape, and divulge his information on the nuclear weapon capability to the Allied forces in person.

He worked feverishly on a plan of escape but couldn't get past the interior walls. About an hour after the change of sentry, he would fake an illness. His plan didn't go beyond that point. He thought of Ahab-The-Arab. *Someway, I'll catch that little dummy by surprise and get his rifle. Maybe I'll be able to shoot my way out of here. Sure. Good, Campbell, real good. It's the drugs. They've ruined my mind. I can't think anything through. I'll never make it out of the building, much less out of Iraq. I've got to try something. I'd rather die while I'm still aware of what's going on around me. I'm not going out a heroin addict, or whatever-in-the-hell it is they're pumping into me.*

Where are our planes? It looks like they didn't break the code. I can't stand it. I'll take as many of 'em as I can with me if I can get my hands on a weapon.

He looked up at the ceiling of his room. *I'm sorry, Grandfather. I know it's stupid, but I've gotta do it. Hear me, please. I can't stay here. If I must die, I want to do it as a whole, sane man. If you learn of my death from these people, you will know what really happened. I will have died the death of a true warrior. Our people will have no reason to be ashamed of me. Explain to Grandmother. If you explain, I know she will understand.*

CHAPTER 4

"Rise and shine. Reveille. Hit the deck. We've got work to do."

Buzz groaned. "What time is it? I'm tired as hell. I don't even know what day it is. What say we get a few more hours rack time? We can hit it again in the morning." He closed his eyes.

Wyman's conversation with General Lewendoski rang his ears. There wasn't much time. He looked at Buzz, sleeping on the floor. *I want to be here to see that it gets done.* He came off the edge of the sofa and grabbed Buzz by the collar of his freshly starched and wrinkled uniform. He pulled him up from the floor and shouted into his face, only an inch from his own. "It *is* morning. And let me tell you something else, Mister. If you've got one little inkling of a code, you don't even think about sleeping. That man," He pointed to the blank tv screen. "is the best fucking friend I've got in this world, not to mention the fact that he might be trying to tell us something of extreme military importance. Don't tell *me* you're too damned tired to work on the code. You hear me, Mister?"

Buzz was suddenly wide-awake. He sat up stiffly "I'm sorry, *Major*. If you order me to work, I don't have a problem with that. I *do* have a problem with you putting your hands on me, *Sir*."

Wyman released his grip slowly and looked away from Buzz. He walked to the other side of the room. "I apologize," he said softly.

"I beg your pardon, sir?"

Wyman raised his voice. "I said I apologize, goddamnit. And quit callin' me sir."

Buzz smiled. "That's better, Bob. Now, where were we?"

Wyman grinned from ear to ear. "I swear. I don't know

how to read you. You're either the dumbest sonofabitch I ever met, or you're the smartest. You want a drink?"

"I thought we covered this ground once before. Where you gonna find booze around here?"

Wyman opened up a small handbag and withdrew a bottle of bourbon. "Right here in this room. I was lying before about not wanting to cause some kind of international incident. I had to be sure of who you were. How do you like it?"

"Water and ice."

"Where you from?"

"Alexandria, Virginia."

"One bourbon and water coming up."

"What's that got to do with anything?" asked Buzz.

"I don't know that it does. I'm just getting into this code business. I'm checking out all the angles."

"Where you from, Bob?"

"Sacramento. That tell you anything?"

"Yeah. It tells me probably drink your bourbon with coke."

Wyman looked at him, an eyebrow raised. "Half and half. How'd you know that?"

"If there's one state in the union where people ruin good whiskey, it's California."

"You know, you could be real dangerous if you really took the time to think about it." He handed Buzz his drink.

Buzz sat it on the floor next to him. "Now, don't bother me. I'm running the tape again. Let's see if we can pick something else out of this."

The first grey light of the day struggled into the room around the corners of the blinds in the windows. "We got any more gedunk?" asked Buzz.

Wyman rubbed his bloodshot eyes. "We don't have anymore anything except a jolt or two of bourbon. You want me to run over to the mess hall and grab us something?"

"Naw, I can wait," said Buzz, a tired smile on his face; a pile of notes on the floor in front of him.

"You want to take a break? I've reached the point where I'm rum-dum already."

"Not yet. I'm running down a series of numbers." He picked up some of the notes and moved to the portable computer on the bed. "It's nice to work for a rich uncle who can afford all of these fancy gadgets. Sure shortens the job."

Wyman watched as Buzz punched in several commands. The little computer whirred noisily. The screen filled with a series of numbers. Buzz studied them carefully. Wyman looked at them but he had no idea what he was seeing. He hoped Buzz did.

"You see anything that makes any sense?"

Buzz shook his head. "Not yet."

"What the hell are you looking for?"

"I'm trying to tie the blinking of the left and right eye to 'Tom' and 'Red'. None of it makes any sense yet, except that when he blinks his right eye, that means 'Red'; the left eye means 'Tom'. I don't get it. Why a 'Red' here and two 'Toms' there?"

"Nothing is beginning to make any sense to me at this point."

Buzz yawned. "I'm in complete agreement with that."

"You gonna be able to hack it?" asked Wyman.

Buzz arched an eyebrow. "You ordered me to, didn't you?"

Wyman grinned. *I like this kid.* "So I did. So I did."

While Buzz played and re-played the tape, Wyman studied the service records of Redd and Posner. Shortly before noon chow, Buzz stopped the tape. "Bob, look at this!"

Wyman shook his head to clear his thoughts and moved next to the machine. "What is it? Whatcha got?"

"We're so stupid."

"No shit. So what we got?"

"Look. I'll roll the tape in slow motion. Watch when he gives his date of birth. See? He blinks with his right eye as he says January; no blink when he says the date, and his right eye again when he says the year. Now, we move on to his service number. He says it real slow. Now, watch. One blink with his left eye on the first number. One right on the second, none on the third, one left on the fourth and so on."

"So what the hell does that mean? Maybe his eyes hurt."

Buzz put the tape on normal speed. "Watch. If you see him blink one more time, let me know."

Wyman watched the tape closely. It ran its course and Buzz shut it off. "I'll be damned. He didn't blink even once. That must have killed him." He faced Buzz squarely. "So have you got it solved?"

Buzz smiled a tired smile. "I wish. I'm a little closer, but I'm still a long way from home."

Wyman mumbled, "Goddamn. One of the most important jobs I've ever been on, and they assign a boot brown-bar to help me out."

Buzz smiled again. "You're a major. How come you haven't figured it out yet?"

Wyman ignored him. "What do you suppose 'Red' and 'Tom' represent?"

"Numbers or progressions."

"Numbers?" asked Wyman.

"Sure. He's altering the numbers he's given us. All we have to do is tie numbers to those names and we're there."

"How do you get numbers out of 'Tom' and 'Red'? The number in the alphabet?"

Buzz shook his head. "Tried that hours ago as part of another sequence. If we use the same data on the dates and serial numbers it doesn't make any sense."

"What about his hands? Do they tie in?"

"I don't see how," answered Buzz. "The key is in the names. They represent a change in the numbers, an unknown amount, in an unknown direction."

Wyman sat heavily on the sofa and wiped his hands down

his face. "How can we be so close and not see it?"

"We could come up with it at any second."

"Or never, right?"

Buzz nodded.

Wyman closed his eyes hard and stared into the blackness. Several minutes passed, neither man speaking. Wyman opened his eyes. "Buzz! I've got it!"

"You've got it? Just like that?"

"Tom and Red – I know who they are."

"They're not the men in your squadron?"

Wyman shook his head. He was unable to contain his excitement. He came out of the sofa like a rocket, then bounced up and down on the carpeted floor. "It's Uncle Red and Cousin Tom – Clare's relatives."

"How do they figure in?"

"They're a couple of honest-to-god hillbillies. I mean to tell you, these guys live out in the middle of nowhere. Jim and I went up to visit them with Clare and Sue – up in the hills of Tennessee, just north of Huntsville, Alabama. They make moonshine and hide from revenuers, just like people did during prohibition. I swear to god, it was like something out of a movie."

"Where's the code?" asked Buzz, a look of excitement starting to grow.

"We went fishing."

"That's the code?"

"No, goddamnit. Well, yes, in a way it is. You see, Red and Tom were bragging about who was the better fisherman, so we went to this river and fished all damn day. There were six of us, and the only one who caught any fish was Red. He caught two of the puniest trout I ever saw. Anyway, when it came time to go back to their cabin, Tom reached over and picked up the stringer and it slipped out of his hand. The fish got away."

"How does that give us the code?" Buzz looked totally confused.

Stoney Livingston

Wyman grinned a wide grin. "Ol' Jim started to laughing, and told them boys they should take a basic math course. He said, 'Plus two for Red and minus two for Tom equals zero for all of us.' He called 'em 'Plus Two' and 'Minus Two' the rest of the time we were there. When we talk about that weekend, he still refers to them as 'Plus Two' and 'Minus Two'."

Buzz's eyes were as big as quarters. He grabbed a pencil and a piece of paper and turned on the VCR. As the tape played, Buzz jotted down numbers. When it finished, he looked down at his completed work.

"Well?" Wyman couldn't contain his anticipation. *This breaking a code business isn't so boring after all.*

Buzz's smile hid the rest of his face. He handed the paper to Wyman.

Wyman took the paper and read it. "ONE. U238. 51923446. What the hell is the 'one' for?"

"Like you said. He'd give a simple code. The one is for the atomic number 'one'. Hydrogen."

Wyman looked into Buzz's watery and bloodshot eyes. "A Fucking hydrogen bomb? That can't be right. You must have made a mistake. Even if they have atomic weapons, there's no way in hell they've got the hydrogen bomb." He whispered quietly in the stillness of the room.

"Given the parameters under which he had to work, I don't think the code was meant to actually specify a hydrogen bomb as such. I see the 'one' as a symbol to represent nuclear weapons; one that would fit into his code and that we could understand in general terms."

"Nukes in general, is that what you're saying?"

Buzz nodded.

"And Jim told us exactly where they are?"

Again Buzz nodded. "Right on the money."

Wyman turned to the phone. "Let's call the general and set up a meeting. I've got an F-18 full of bombs waiting for me on the

Coral Sea."

"It won't happen until we've identified the target."

"Identified the target? Hell, Jim did that. He told us what they have and where it is. What else do we need to know?"

"There are still a few things to be checked out. I imagine you'll get your chance, but it won't be this afternoon. I just want you to understand that."

"Okay, okay. Tomorrow morning is good enough for me." Wyman picked up the phone.

Wyman sat in the map room next to Buzz as the latter peered through a stereoscope at aerial photographs of the target area pinpointed by Campbell. Within minutes of their meeting with General Lewendoski, the recon birds had been over the target, taking pictures.

Buzz grunted. He pulled his eyes from the scope. "I don't see anything in these pictures, but that doesn't mean anything. The large building in frame one sixty-three is big enough to be about anything."

"We know what it is. Jim wouldn't have made the kind of statement he did if he wasn't certain."

"What if he has his coordinates wrong?"

Wyman looked at Buzz through one eye. "With his memory? Get real, Buzz. That's the building and we know what it's being used for."

"You heard the navy commander. Everything we've got on that building says it's a civilian milk plant."

"They're wrong, goddamnit. It's a front. Saddamn Hussein is an asshole. He'll do anything to protect himself. I wouldn't be surprised to see him attack us in planes marked with red crosses."

Buzz glanced at his watch. "We've got time for chow before the meeting. You hungry?"

"I'm hungry as hell but I don't feel like eating. You go. I'll stay and see if anything new comes in before the briefing."

Buzz shook his head. "You're as heard-headed as any man I ever met."

"Wait till you meet Jim."

Buzz looked away.

"He'll be back," said Wyman confidently.

Buzz turned back to him. "He's kind of in a no win situation, Bob. If the brass buys his code and we take out the target, he's a dead man. If we don't – who knows what they're doing to him?"

Wyman's hopes sank. He knew what Buzz said was a fact, but in the excitement of breaking the code he had lost touch with reality for a short time. He looked at his watch. "I guess you're right – we might as well grab some chow."

The briefing room was silent as General Lewendoski stepped into the room and seated himself at the head of the table. "Be seated, gentlemen."

The shuffle of bodies and the creaking of chairs took only a few seconds from the briefing. General Lewendoski cleared his throat. He glanced at Buzz and Wyman, then let his eyes roam the table. "Gentlemen, as you all know, Captain Campbell's message to us was rather succinct. We would like to have had a few more details but, under the circumstances, he did well sending what he did.

"With the exception of Major Wyman here," he nodded, "all of you know our verification procedure on information of this nature." He faced to his left. "Commander Boswell, what have we got here?"

Boswell cleared his throat and shuffled a sheaf of papers on the table in front of him. He picked up the papers and moved to the large map behind him. With a pointer, he indicated a position on the large-scale map. "The coordinates sent by Captain Campbell put the facility right here on this map." He indicated a small circle with his pointer. "If this facility is producing nuclear weapons, there are certain criteria which must be met in order to do so with any semblance of proficiency and safety.

"The availability of water to cool the reactors is one consideration." He turned to an enlarged aerial photo to the right of the map and pointed to a small outbuilding near a larger building. "This appears to be a pumping station of sorts. I know those of you assigned to this unit are still working on confirmation but, it looks like, at this point, it *is* a high-capacity cooling system."

The pointer moved to a larger structure, about four hundred yards south of the main plant. "This building here," He tapped the photograph. "is an auxiliary electrical generating station, of that we have no doubt." He glanced at an Air Force major. "Is that right, Major Benson?" Benson nodded and Boswell continued. "This generating station has the capability to support a city the size of Yuma, Arizona with twice the power it would need at peak hours – another indication that we're dealing with something other than a milk plant."

Wyman fidgeted in his chair. *Why the hell doesn't he just get down to brass tacks? Do we target this plant or not?*

The pointer moved east and on line with the main plant. It stopped at the river only a quarter-mile from the building. "Here, if policy allowed, is a means for disposing of some of the less hazardous by-products of nuclear reactors. And here..." The pointer traced a barely discernable line on the ground from the main plant to the river. "...is a pipe that is not needed for normal sewage disposal since the sewer line is up here." He pointed and traced another line to the river.

"The fact that there is a sizeable pumping station located so close to a river of this size is cause to question the purpose of the facility. Given the other factors already mentioned, I'm of the opinion that Captain Campbell may well be correct in his assessment of the plant located here."

Boswell turned to Lewendoski. The latter said, "Thank you, Commander." He looked to the far end of the table. "Colonel

Bains."

A tall, lanky Army lieutenant colonel moved crisply to the map and aerial photo. He picked up the pointer and said, "Good afternoon, gentlemen." His pointer tapped the map. "Here you see the top of the building. Notice that, despite its size, it does not show as clearly as some of the much smaller surrounding buildings."

He pulled a photograph from behind the easel and placed it in front of the large-scale map. "This is an enlargement of the main plant and the area immediately surrounding it. As you can see, extensive work has been done to the top of the building to render it difficult to see from the air. They've painted it in camouflage and added trees so that it appears at first glance to look like a small oasis from above."

He moved his pointer to the upper left-hand corner of the picture. "Note this spot on the photo." He pulled another picture from behind the easel and placed it in front of the enlarged version. "This, gentlemen, is a detailed enlargement of the spot. It's much clearer under a scope than it is on an enlargement, but take my word for it, what we have here is an anti-aircraft position." Bains exposed the previous photo. "Now that you know they're there, you can see several of these spots surrounding the facility. A detailed inspection revealed them all to be anti-aircraft positions."

Bains moved back to the large area photo and motioned a circle of the whole picture. "Gentlemen, there is nothing in this general area to justify the locations of those anti-aircraft positions. We've been able to ascertain no major supply or munitions facilities, nor do we have any evidence of major troop staging. As far as we've been able to determine the only major activity taking place in this area is the production and processing of milk and baby formula."

A murmur made its way around the table. Wyman could no longer contain himself. "So when do we attack the target?"

Desert Fire

Bains nodded to General Lewendoski. "General?"

Lewendoski glanced from Wyman to Bains. "Thank you, Colonel. You may be seated." He faced Wyman. "I know you want a piece of this, Major, but there are several things to address yet." He nodded to an Air Force captain. "Captain Billings."

The short and stocky Billings stepped up to the photograph and picked up the pointer left by Bains. He tapped it in his palm several times. "Gentlemen, suppose for a moment this facility is producing nuclear materials for weapons. Let's further suppose we assault it from the air with pinpoint accuracy and blow it all to hell as Major Wyman and most of the rest of us would like to do." He paused, looking directly into Wyman's eyes. "What if, in the course of our assault, we spread nuclear waste over the area for, say five or ten miles? What are the consequences?"

"Excuse me, sir, but are you saying a nuclear detonation might occur?" asked Buzz.

Billings shook his head. "Not likely, Lieutenant. But the possibility of spreading radiation over a wide area as the result of the conventional bombing is high."

Billings turned back to the detailed enlargement. "It is possible to make a 'best guess' as to where the nuclear materials are located in the building using means I won't go into at this briefing and, by using laser-guided missiles, avoid a direct hit in that area. We could assault the target in a manner designed to cause its collapse onto itself and diminish the possibility of radiation leakage." He faced Lewendoski. "General?"

"Thank you, Captain." Lewendoski let his eyes roam the men in the room. "Gentlemen, the possibility that we have a priority target here is great but, unfortunately, I can't recommend it as such."

Wyman leaned forward in his chair.

Lewendoski held up a hand. "Think about it, Major. The ramifications if we made a mistake could alter the sentiment of the American public. The Commander-in-Chief isn't going to take a chance that we might bomb a baby milk processing plant on circumstantial evidence and the word of one man. We don't even know that Campbell is qualified to recognize nuclear weapons in the manufacturing stage."

Wyman felt his frustration building. "Maybe it's a staging area for nukes, sir."

"That makes it an even closer call, Major."

"I know Captain Campbell very well, Sir. And I know there are nuclear weapons at that facility. What do we have to have before we go after it?"

"Corroboration, Major. From a trusted and qualified source."

Wyman stared into the general's eyes. "Where the hell do we find that in the middle of the damn desert, in enemy-held territory, sir?"

Lewendoski shook his head. "I don't know, Major. I don't know." He glanced about the table. "That will do it for now. With the exception of Major Wyman, who is reporting back to his unit tomorrow, I want you all here at 0800." He stood.

A lieutenant on the general's staff shouted. "Ten-hut!"

The general stood and left the room.

Wyman remained seated, twirling a pencil in his hand. He felt a hand on his shoulder.

"Have you got a minute, Major?" It was Captain Billings.

Wyman nodded.

Buzz tapped him on the other shoulder. "I'll see you outside."

"That's okay, Lieutenant. You can stay." Billings sat in the vacated chair on Wyman's right.

"What's up?" asked Wyman, almost disinterestedly.

"It's not as hopeless as you might think."

Wyman sighed. "Yeah, maybe not, but it sure as hell isn't looking too rosy. I don't want this thing turned into another Vietnam anymore than anybody else does. The president needs the support of the public. If they even think we bombed a baby milk plant, every do-gooder in the world will be out to destroy the war effort." Wyman curled his lip in a sinister smile. "Maybe Jane Fonda could come over and give 'em moral support and help re-arm the bastards."

"That was a long time ago."

"She hasn't served any time for it yet."

"Don't hold your breath on that one," said Buzz.

"I won't." He looked up at Billings. "You got any ideas, Captain?"

"Not ideas, but hope. There's still a chance we'll get corroboration. We have people in Iraq. And there is some resistance, though it's small. There are a bunch of people that haven't forgiven Saddam Hussein for using chemical weapons on his own people." He stood and patted Wyman on the back. "That's all I wanted to say, Captain. Our chance may come yet. Don't give up the faith."

"Thanks, Captain. I appreciate it."

Wyman sat up in his bed, staring into the darkness of his room, contemplating the events of the past several days. He felt small and insignificant in the overall scheme of events taking place around him. He looked at the darkness where Buzz slept on the other bed in the small room. *Hell, he plays a bigger part in the total picture than I do. Me, with my four North Vietnamese MIGS to my credit. One more and I'm an ace. Probably the only one left on active duty. So what? I wanted that fifth plane so bad I could taste it when this whole thing started. That's all it was to me was a big game. I'd still like to have the fifth kill, but only so my kids, if I ever get married, can say their dad was an ace fighter pilot. Other than that, what good is it to be an ace?*

"You awake, Bob?"

Buzz's voice startled him. He spun his head in the direction of the sound. When his heart slowed down, he said, "Yeah, I'm awake. What are you doin' still awake?"

"Same as you I guess – waiting for another day to get started."

"It doesn't make sense, Buzz. This whole thing doesn't make sense. The war's been draggin' on, and we're kicking ass and takin' names, and we worry about blowing up one more building. What the hell difference would it make? Even if it turned out to be a damn milk factory, we have every damn reason in the world to take it out. Jim may have given his life to pass us a code that we break and then do nothing about. It doesn't make any sense."

"Staying awake isn't going to make any major changes in how things are," said Buzz.

"Yeah, I know, Buzz, but I've just been running a few things through my mind and I wonder if the day will ever come when men stop fighting wars. What will all the soldiers, airmen, sailors and marines do? Hell, we need wars to keep part of our population employed. Saddam Hussein needed another war to focus his people's attention away from the fact that he's dumber than a bucket of shit when it comes to running a country. All he knows how to do is kill people. And when he's confronted by a decent foe, he can't even do that very well."

"You're right, Bob, but there isn't anything we can do about it tonight."

"I can think about it, goddamnit."

CHAPTER 5

Buzz watched motionlessly as the helicopter slowly faded to a dark dot in the sky and disappeared. During the few days he had been with Major Bob Wyman, he had grown to like the man – really like him. He wasn't Major Wyman to him, just "Bob", and nothing more. He would always be Bob – Bob, the great guy – Bob, the seasoned veteran – Bob, the guy with a deep devotion to a downed pilot – Bob, the go-getter, patriotic American – Bob, the only guy in the camp with a bottle of American bourbon – and Bob, the man with a burning desire to shoot down an Iraqi jet.

Buzz smiled at the empty sky. *I'll never see another F-18 without thinking of you and your buddy, you hard-nosed old phoney.* He turned and walked back to the room. Bob was there everywhere – the chewing gum wrappers, the tightly made bed, the whiskey label taped to a notepad. Buzz stuffed the notepad into his briefcase.

He sat on the small sofa and stared at the blank television screen. *What the hell am I doing here? I should be flying with you, Bob, old man.* He glanced from the TV screen to the flat terrain outside the window. *You know, Bob, all this was to me when I first started the mission was a chance to break the big one; to finally be known as Lieutenant Geoffrey Griswold – not "Skip's boy". Damnit all, Bob, now you want me to ask him to go to bat for me, just like he did when I was a kid and got into more trouble than I could handle.* He would never forget Bob's parting remark.

"Your old man has a lot of pull, even if he isn't a general.

I'm asking you to use your influence and convince him to tell the brass we need to bomb the hell out of that milk plant."

Buzz leaned back in the sofa and stared at the ceiling. *I'll do it, Pal. But if we ever meet again, you owe me big time, you sonafabitch.* He felt the tears running down his cheeks and closed his eyes tightly shut.

He heard his father's words and saw his face as he spoke. "Are you sure this is what you want to do? You're not doing it just to please me? I want you to make a choice that you can live with, and I don't want to be accused later of influencing your decision."

Buzz had avoided his father's gaze. "Dad, I'm twenty years old. I can make my own decisions. This has nothing to do with you. I figure when I graduate next year, I can go to Officer's Candidate School, get a commission and serve my time. If I don't like it, I can leave after my obligation is up. And if I like it, at least I'll be an officer."

Lieutenant Colonel Skip Griswold had smiled. "Being an officer isn't all it's cracked up to be." He paused. "But now that I think about it, it *is* better than being enlisted. Too many stupid officers ordering you around."

Buzz knew the story of his father's rise through the ranks from private to lieutenant colonel. His father was proud of his service record, and rightfully so. It isn't just any man who can command an infantry battalion with no more formal education than high school to his credit. *Yeah, Dad, but if you had a college degree, you'd be a general by now.* "That's my way of thinking, Dad. So what do you think?"

Skip had put his arm around his son's shoulders. "I think it's a damn good idea. Now, who's going to tell your mama?"

Buzz couldn't remember the time when his father had acted unfairly. Sure, there had been times when he had been strict in his discipline but, if the truth were known, Buzz got away with more than enough to make up for the few times his father had punished him.

Buzz's clean-cut good looks made him a favorite with the girls, starting way back in junior high school. When he was a freshman in high school, he got his first taste of what manhood meant. His date that night had been with Mary Jo Swan, a senior. Mary Jo taught him a few things about biology that night, things not taught in biology 101a.

At first, Buzz thought he was in love but he soon found himself attracted to other girls and, with his newfound knowledge and confidence, he gave more than his share of biology lessons to the girls on campus. A scandal in his junior year forced his father to remove him from public school and place him in a military academy until his graduation more than a year later.

Buzz's entry into the Marine Corps was a major step. Unlike many young men his age who joined to serve their time as painlessly as possible in the officer's club, Buzz looked upon his commission as a first step. He wasn't sure where the steps would lead but he was certain he would build on his experience, even if he resigned his commission when his obligation was fulfilled.

When the results of his aptitude tests were interpreted, Buzz had several options opened to him. He considered applying for flight school but the Marine Corps had more helicopter and fighter pilots than it did transport pilots. If his time served was going to be a building block, flying in the Corps was out. His chances of being assigned to transports were slim. In civilian life, the airlines much preferred transport pilots with hundreds of hours of multi-engine time to fighter jet jockeys or helicopter pilots with thousands of hours behind the stick. Flying in the Corps was *definitely* out.

Buzz couldn't see himself as an infantry officer. Despite the infantry being the heart of the Marine Corps, it was also his father's field. He wanted his own identity. When a classmate at O.C.S. suggested intelligence training, Buzz jumped at the chance. He had never thought about it before.

Stoney Livingston

Buzz found he had a penchant for codes, electronic equipment and clandestine operations. On his second month at his first duty station in the Pentagon, he had broken a complex voice code using synthesizers and a mainframe computer. His decoded message was instrumental in preventing a terrorist attack on a naval station in Rota, Spain. Still, senior officers who knew his father referred to him as "Skip's boy", a title which rankled him. He was his own man. When would they give him his own name?

The phone jarred Buzz out of his reverie. He snatched up the receiver. "Lieutenant Griswold."

"Lieutenant, this is General Lewendoski. Can you report to my office in thirty minutes?"

He's *asking* *me to report? What kind of a deal is this? I didn't expect this much respect for decoding Campbell's message.* "I can be there in ten minutes, sir."

"That'll be fine, Lieutenant." The phone went dead.

What the hell was that all about? He hung up the phone and stepped into the bathroom. After placing his pisscutter squarely on his head and brushing out the wrinkles in his uniform blouse, he picked up his briefcase and walked briskly to the general's office.

The sergeant at the desk outside the general's door smiled. "Good morning, Lieutenant. The general's expecting you. Go right on in."

Buzz was confused as he stepped past the sergeant and opened the door. Inside the room, he saw the general sitting behind his large desk. Buzz brought himself to stiff attention in front of Lewendoski. "Lieutenant Griswold reporting as ordered, sir."

Lewendoski waved casually at the chair next to Buzz. "At ease, Lieutenant. Have a seat. I'll be with you in just a second."

"Yessir." Buzz sat in the chair and waited for the general to complete whatever it was he was doing with a set of papers.

72

Desert Fire

After a moment, Lewendoski placed the papers in a neat stack and looked up at Buzz. "How does that name suit you?"

"Name, sir?"

"That one Major Wyman called you – Buzz. You seem to have taken to it."

Buzz shrugged. *This is irregular as hell. What's he leading up to?* "It's as good a name as any, sir. Most of the men in the Corps have a nickname. If I gotta have one, that one suits me fine."

"Well, Buzz, that isn't really why I called you to my office."

Buzz squirmed in his seat. "I didn't think it was, sir."

"There's an officer on his way to my office right now with a set of silver bars for you. You got here a little quicker than I thought you would, but he should be here shortly. You won't have long to wait. I'd give 'em to you myself but I know how you leathernecks are about tradition." Lewendoski smiled. "The fella carrying those bars in is a legend, even for you damn marines."

"May I ask..."

"Ten-hut!" said Lewendoski.

Buzz snapped to attention, nearly knocking his chair over in the process. He kept his eyes straight to the front, boring a hole in the wall behind the general's desk.

Lewendoski spoke to the newcomer. "Colonel. It's good to see you. Glad you could make it for this occasion. May I introduce you to Lieutenant Geoffrey 'Buzz' Griswold?"

"Buzz?"

Buzz knew the voice. A mixture of pride and disappointment swept through him.

"At ease, Lieutenant," said Lewendoski. "Lieutenant, I believe you know the colonel."

Buzz turned around and looked into his father's smiling face. "Hi, Dad." Father and son hugged each other tightly.

Skip backed away and took in his son's appearance. "You look mighty fit, *Buzz*."

73

Buzz felt the heat rise to his ears as his nickname rolled off his father's tongue. "It's just a name a pilot gave me. He's a helluva guy, Dad. You'd like him."

"Well, I sure as hell like the handle he planted on you. I think it's great." Skip's smile was genuine.

"Are you serious?"

Skip clucked his tongue and shook his head. "Do you know how damned irritating it is to have someone ask me, 'How's your son doing?' It's like they can't remember your name for Christ sake. I swear, if my exec does it one more time, I'll have him transferred to Twenty-Nine Palms as a perimeter guard. With a name like 'Buzz', he won't forget it, especially when I tell him it was none other than Pappy Wyman who gave it to you."

"Pappy? Pappy? He doesn't look that old to me."

Skip laughed. "For a fighter jock, he's ancient. Still one of the best in the sky though."

"For crying out loud, do all of you damn marines know one another?" asked Lewendoski.

Skip turned to him. "Forgive me, General." They shook hands. "This is a special day in more ways than one. I think I'm more excited about the damned identity crisis being solved than I am the promotion." He turned back to Buzz. "I'm sorry, son. I know a promotion is important, especially the one that lets you get rid of those damn gold bars – most embarrassing rank I ever held – but I don't think you know what a relief it is to me that someone finally put a name on you that fits. I told your mom when you were in grade school I thought we should have given you a name with more pzazz."

Buzz stood dumbly. The promotion buried in the back of his mind. He was no longer "Skip's boy." He was lieutenant Buzz Griswold. *Hell, I may even have it legally changed.* "Yeah, it does kind of have a ring to it, doesn't it?"

Skip and the general smiled warmly.

"Let's get on with this promotion. I'm sure you two have

some catching up to do before you have to return to your regiment, Colonel."

"Right. Yessir." Skip reached casually into his trouser pocket and withdrew a shiny set of silver bars while Lewendoski picked up a paper from the top of the stack on his desk.

Buzz looked at Lewendoski and held up a hand. "Excuse me, sir, but you may not want to see the Marine Corps promote me after I tell you what I was going to do." He felt the butterflies in his stomach. There was no quicker way. He had them both in the same room at the same time.

His father looked at him quizzically. The general held the papers at his waist.

"What is it, Lieutenant? I have nothing to do with promotions in the Marine Corps." Lewendoski pointed to his collar. "You won't see a globe and anchor on these collars."

"I'd like you to hear me out first, sir." Buzz turned to his father. "You too, dad."

"What is it, son?"

Buzz looked at Lewendoski. "May we be seated, sir? This could take a few minutes."

The general motioned to the chairs in the room. "Make yourself comfortable."

After the two senior officers were seated, Buzz sat and opened his briefcase. He pulled out a thick file folder and placed it on the desk in front of him, then looked Lewendoski square in the eyes. "Sir, fortune – good or bad – has saved me a lot of time and soul-searching.

"I was going to try to set up a meeting with my father and have him use what influence he might have to force an air strike against the target revealed by Captain Campbell." Buzz nodded in his father's direction. "The fact that he showed up here to pin the silver bars on my uniform is a sign to me that what I am doing now is the only way to approach this subject. I was..."

"Lieutenant, perhaps you might want to address this issue

at a later time. I'm sure with the excitement of decoding the message, your promotion, and the arrival of your father, your emotions are a bit high."

Buzz looked from the general to his father, who sat stoically in his chair. He turned back to Lewendoski. "No, sir. If you'll permit me, I'd like to go on."

Lewendoski glanced at Skip. The latter shrugged. "I've got faith in him, sir. Let him proceed."

Lewendoski nodded.

"Thank you, sir," said Buzz. "Sir, I am thoroughly convinced that Captain Campbell made an accurate assessment of the facility at the specified coordinates. I am also of the opinion that we must take advantage of the first-strike opportunity afforded us by Captain Campbell's information – provided to us at no small risk to himself."

Lewendoski shook his head slowly. "Lieutenant, I can understand your zeal and enthusiasm, but this decision is not yours to make. The information has been passed through the proper channels and will be acted upon by those in a position authorized to make decisions of this magnitude."

"Sir, give me the argument against striking the target." Buzz felt embarrassment as he heard the pleading tone in his voice.

Lewendoski hesitated. He gave an apologetic look to Skip, who remained stoic in his appearance, and turned back to face Buzz. "Lieutenant," his voice had a harsher tone. "There are too many factors involved to discuss at this time. We don't know how Campbell got his information, nor how reliable it is. We don't know if he can positively differentiate between a nuclear- electrical generating station and a nuclear weapons facility. We have no idea of his ability to memorize the subtle differences between peaceful nukes and weaponry. He may have..."

Buzz stood. "Sir, begging the general's pardon, but there probably isn't a man more qualified in the world than Captain

Campbell to identify a nuclear weapon – probably to build them for that matter."

Skip leaned forward in his chair. "Sit down, Buzz. You're an officer in the Corps. I needn't remind you of proper deportment."

Buzz turned to his father. "Damnit, dad, in addition to an I.Q. of 165, Campbell graduated from the University of New Mexico State with an engineering degree in Aerospace. And the man has a photographic memory."

"He has a what?" asked Lewendoski.

"A photographic memory, sir. From what I understand, a perfect one. He can recall anything he's ever seen or read with one hundred percent accuracy."

Lewendoski cleared his throat. "I didn't see anything in his SRB about a photographic memory, Lieutenant. Where did you get your information?"

"From a reliable source, sir."

"That won't wash in this room, Lieutenant. You're no damn newspaperman. I asked you a question and I want a straight answer."

It was out in the open. There was no point in wasting time. "Major Wyman, sir."

Lewendoski squinted one eye. "Major Wyman told you this man had a photographic memory?"

Buzz nodded. "Yessir."

Lewendoski looked to Skip. "How well do you know this Major Wyman, Colonel?"

"Not very well on a personal basis but what little I know of him is all good. In '70, I thought he was going to land an A-4 in the middle of the damn jungle. I was commanding a rifle company at the time. One of my platoons got cut off by a large unit of North Vietnamese Regulars. It was close to dark and we had no artillery support. Ammo was low.

"All of a sudden this damn little Skyhawk dropped out of the blue and laid one on those gooks like I've never seen it done before or since. The pilot dropped what heavy ordinance he had and asked my platoon leader if he could hold out another hour or so. When my man said his ammo wouldn't last ten more minutes, the pilot hung over the area, strafing the gooks with his machineguns as the platoon fought its way out. He came in so low a couple of times, one of the squad sergeants claimed the A-4 took out two of the gooks with its wingtips.

The platoon finally made it to within range of our artillery and the A-4 made one last pass. He ran out of ammo about midway in his run and put that damn bird about ten feet off the deck. What few gooks were still in pursuit of my platoon buried themselves in the mud. He scared the hell out of 'em without any functional weaponry.

"I busted a few channels to find out who the pilot was and, when I found out, I paid him a visit with my platoon commander. Had to make some special arrangements to get out to his carrier but we got the job done. Turned out it was Wyman. Helluva a pilot and a helluva guy. He's no dummy. If he says Campbell's got a photographic memory, then I believe the man's got a photographic memory."

Lewendoski tapped a pencil on his desktop and contemplated the marks on the wall behind Skip. He looked at Buzz, then to Skip. "This *does* put a different light on things."

Skip shook his head. "I wouldn't want to have your responsibilities, sir. Give me a regiment of Marine infantry any time."

Lewendoski faced Buzz. "Why is it none of this is in his service record book, Lieutenant? Did Major Wyman explain that to you?"

Buzz nodded. "Yessir."

"What was that, Lieutenant? I didn't hear you."

Buzz cleared his throat. "Yessir."

Lewendoski arched his eyebrows. "Well, Lieutenant, I'm

78

waiting."

"Well, sir..." Buzz paused. He tried to think of a diplomatic way of putting it, but couldn't find one. "Apparently, Captain Campbell chose to hide his ability from the Corps. He wanted to fly fighter jets; not be a spy or some kind of secret weapon."

Lewendoski raised his eyebrows almost to his hairline.

"Those aren't my words, sir."

Lewendoski faced Skip. "Colonel, are you able to remain here for a few more hours? I'd like to call a staff meeting and I'd like you to be there."

Skip nodded, the stoic look gone from his face. Buzz thought he detected the beginnings of a faint smile as his father said, "It will be my privilege, sir."

CHAPTER 6

Campbell awakened to the crash of a muffled explosion from somewhere above him in the building. Without his watch, he wasn't sure of the time, but he thought it somewhere around 0100. His plan to fake an illness ran through his mind. The building shook and vibrated from another explosion. The late wail of an air raid siren reached him.

A fragment of cement larger than a good-sized sports car careened down the long hall, taking the wall of Campbell's room out as it continued to its final resting place at the end of the corridor.

Campbell spent only a fraction of a second assessing the damage, then charged into the hall. The mangled body of Ahab, his guard, lay in the debris on the floor. The man's arm upon which he had worn the watch was missing from the shoulder, blood still gushing in spurts from the gaping wound left by the severed appendage. Campbell stared at the blood for a few seconds, until the gushing stopped. The man's heart was no longer beating.

"Damn!" Campbell charged down the hall, searching for a weapon and a way out. Explosions continued to rock the building. In places, the bulkheads had collapsed, allowing the upper floors to fall to the lower level, blocking hallways and filling rooms. A blast ripped the air above him, sending tons of debris into the hallway. He cringed against a wall. As the dust settled, Campbell lifted a "thumbs up" and issued a silent cheer to the unseen Allied pilots. *Good shootin', whoever you are. I wonder who the hell it is. I hope it's Bob or Redd, or one of the other guys in my squadron. That would be almost too sweet.*

Near his feet was a severed arm. On the wrist was his watch. For a moment he knelt and studied the lifeless arm. Surely Ahab had pissed off the spirits by stealing his watch and this was the payback. Quickly he removed the watch from the bloody arm and placed it on his own wrist, ignoring the blood, looking only to see if it was still running. It was. He took it as a sign, a sign that he would get out of this place and show the watch to his grandparents and tell them this story.

A man stepped out of a nearby room and moved drunkenly in Campbell's direction. *He's unarmed.* Recognition crept into Campbell's brain. *The Air Force major!* Another blast ripped into the floor above and Campbell watched helplessly as a large beam and tons of heavy flooring buried the major alive. Campbell climbed the pile of rubble and tore at it frantically but it was hopeless. His efforts to remove the debris had no better effect than a single termite's attempt at razing a house alone. He rolled down the steep slope of concrete and steel and moved dazedly down the hall, tears dimming his vision. He cursed Saddam Hussein under his breath.

He found two dead soldiers near a laboratory, their weapons strewn about the hall, their bodies grotesquely mangled and disfigured. He picked up an AK-47, several magazines of ammo and four hand grenades. With newfound fighting power in his hands he searched more confidently for a way out of the complex.

Three soldiers raced around a corner at the end of the hallway in front of him. Campbell fired a ten-round burst from his AK-47 and watched through the concrete dust as they crumpled to the floor. He charged forward to finish his work but found he had done his job well and no further action was necessary. He picked up two more automatic rifles, three more hand grenades and a survival knife from the bodies.

Another explosion rocked the building. The lights flickered

twice, then there was almost total darkness. Campbell felt his way down the hall and searched for a way that would lead him to the ground above. He heard voices in front of him. He pulled the pin on one of his grenades and lobbed it in the direction of the sounds. In the flash that accompanied the explosion, he saw three men dressed in lab smocks crumple to the floor, then darkness.

Damn! That was stupid. Now I've lost my night vision for a minute or two. Not that it's much help down here. I wonder how far underground I am?

One of the men injured in the grenade blast moaned loudly. Campbell held his breath and advanced down the hallway slowly. The injured man spoke in a pleading tone.

Damn! I wish I could understand this lingo.

The two automatic rifles on his back made a metallic sound as the barrels fell against each other. Campbell held his advance and waited.

He heard movement in the darkness ahead. An explosion ripped into the floor overhead, dumping the contents of the rooms above into the hallway. A scream was cut short by tons of falling concrete. Campbell retreated back down the hall as the smoke and dust filled his lungs.

The sound of anti-aircraft fire was louder. The last explosion had blown a passage to the ground above. Campbell inched forward, crawling over the jagged edges of concrete and broken furniture. Tracers filled the night sky as the Iraqi gunners fired into the darkness. He clambered to the top of the heap of rubble and stepped into the night air.

An anti-aircraft gun boomed projectiles into the night only fifty yards from where he stood. Campbell pulled the pins on three of his hand grenades and rushed to the enemy gun in a low crouch, holding the spoons in place. At the base of the parapet, he tossed the grenades into the gunpit and threw himself to the ground. A grin washed his face. *Just like we practiced it in*

Recon. In the ensuing flashes from the explosions, he spotted an Armored Personnel Carrier.

With his captured weapons clattering on his back, he ran to the unattended machine. Another missile struck the laboratory. A chunk of concrete from the building whizzed overhead and slammed into the APC with such force that it almost turned the vehicle over. It was still rocking when he opened the door. He fumbled in the darkness until he found the ignition switch, with the key in place, and the engine roared to life at the twist of his wrist.

The pungent smell of burnt powder wafted into his nostrils. He glanced at the confusion that surrounded him. *They don't even know I'm out here. They must think their gun was hit by the planes.* A freshly painted sign leaned against a chain-link fence. Campbell glanced at the picture of a baby drinking milk from a bottle. *Who the hell are they kidding? A baby milk factory? That's a good one.*

He closed his eyes and visualized the map of the compound he had seen in the briefing room, then opened them and drove through the confusion around him and onto the main highway. He headed south, the bombs and missiles still raining down on the nuclear laboratory; the Iraqi gunners still firing into the nothingness above.

Campbell grinned as the Iraqi vehicle rumbled down the road. He shouted in the isolation of the noisy cab of the APC. "Whoever you are, that's damn good shootin'. Take one more out for me." He paused and looked skyward. "I just wish to hell you hadn't blown that guy's arm off. My watch could have gotten busted. You gotta be more careful about collateral damage in the future."

The engine sputtered once, then twice. It coughed violently, then, like a mortally wounded soldier, it died quietly, without celebration. Campbell pulled the APC to the shoulder of the road and sat quietly for a moment. *Only four-hours-worth of fuel?*

He stared into a black sky, the slight overcast blocking out the stars. The vehicle sat silent and unmoving. He pounded on the steering wheel and silently beseeched the heavens above for a sign. *Where is everybody? Is there still a USA out there somewhere? Where are you guys? Are you all okay? Has the ground war started yet? Which way should I go?*

He knew whichever way he went, he would have to continue on foot. He had been lucky to get this far without interference from the Iraqis. His plan to abandon the vehicle right away had disappeared from his mind as he sped down an empty highway. He estimated he had covered almost two-hundred miles in his stolen vehicle and had seen not a sign of life..

He looked down at the half-full canteen in his hands. It wasn't much but it would have to do. He turned and searched for more supplies in the cabin but had no success. The Iraqi helmet would be no use. *That's all I need to do is give 'em an excuse to shoot me as a spy – not that they need much of an excuse for anything.*

He stepped into the cool desert air, wishing first that he had a cigarette, then that he was back in New Mexico having dinner with an American woman – any American woman. *A bottle of California Cabernet Sauvignon would sure be nice. And a juicy steak.* His stomach growled. He longed for the mountains of New Mexico. He loved his homeland and his people – not only the Mescaleros, but all Americans. *I'd rather every man, woman, and child in Iraq die than one American. It doesn't make sense to feel that way about an inanimate object, or something as intangible as "country" or "home." How does a man get to feel that way about a country?* He felt a pang of hunger.

The faint sound of jet aircraft reached his ears. *Ours or theirs?* There had been very few Iraqi aircraft in the sky during the first two days of the war. *And what few there were, weren't much of a match for us.* He thought of the downed Mig-29 and smiled. *Odds are those are ours. They had to take me out with a missile. Shit, it doesn't matter. I can't stay here.* Campbell ran into the sand away from the road, putting as much distance between him and the Iraqi APC as quickly as he could. He crested a large dune almost two-hundred yards from the road and fell to the sand, gasping for breath, two of his three automatic rifles still with him; the other lost in his mad dash.

Wyman's radio crackled. "Dusty Leader. At your nine. On the road. Looks like a personnel carrier. Doesn't appear to be moving."

"Roger Dusty two," replied Wyman. "Dusty two, you're the only one who has any ground ordinance left. Take a shot. We'll cover," he ordered, smiling all the while, knowing that Posner had been searching the ground for any target of opportunity to present itself so he could unload his ordinance.

"Take notes, Pappy. I'll show you how it's supposed to be done," said Posner in Dusty two.

Wyman watched the sky for enemy aircraft as Posner made his approach on the Iraqi personnel carrier. He had no need to watch Posner. He knew the man would roll into the target with practiced ease, almost like he was coming in for a landing, then he would release the air-to-ground missile, light up his tail and aim for the sky. Posner loved combat acrobatics. If he wasn't so damned good, Wyman would chastise him, but he was good – about as good as they get.

Campbell crawled back to the crest of the dune and looked toward the road, then skyward. In the darkness it was difficult to see clearly but he thought the approaching aircraft might be F-18s. One of the four aircraft rolled left and slowed as it aimed itself at the APC. As the plane drew nearer, it dropped to almost ground level. At a distance of 1000 yards from the Iraqi vehicle, a missile fired, the jet accelerated and nosed abruptly upward. There was a flash of light and the eerie sounds of irregularly shaped objects whining through the air in all directions as the APC was instantly converted into a disjointed mass of unrelated parts. He smiled a bitter smile at the destruction of his salvation from the Iraqi compound and stifled a cheer only out of fear of being heard by an unseen enemy. He knew by the sound of the accelerating aircraft that it was, indeed, an F-18, and he further knew the pilot was Posner from his own outfit. He was the only man alive who flew ground support that way. He knew too that Bob Wyman was still in command, otherwise, Posner wouldn't have dared to take his "trick" shot. He cast a silent salute to the pilots.

With the glow of the burning truck at his back he walked south – south to Kuwait; south to freedom. The stars told him he had another couple of hours before sunrise and he wanted to be as far from the wreckage as he could get before the sun forced him into hiding.

When he looked to the stars for guidance, he thought of his grandfather first, then survival school. His grandfather had taught him to find his way in the night by using the stars as beacons; survival school had taught him the difference in the stars over New Mexico and those that appeared in this part of the world.

An hour into his trek he heard hammering in the darkness in front of him. He crouched low and advanced in the direction of the noise, the faint light cast by the stars not much help to his vision. From his prone position near the crest of a large dune, he watched as several men nailed and wired large sections of plywood to the sides of a stripped garbage truck. Two small floodlights connected to a generator on the truck supplied power to the lights.

Why in the hell would anyone put plywood on the outside of a garbage truck? He watched for twenty minutes, until the size and shape of the garbage truck changed considerably. *Decoys! They're making dummy SCUD mobile missile launchers!*

Desert Fire

Campbell's heart beat wildly in his chest. *Damn! Some of our guys will get shot out of the sky trying to take out plywood trucks!* He skirted the position and continued south, quickening his pace, more determined than ever before to return to the Allied lines and report what the Iraqis were doing and what their positions were.

The bright glow of the early morning sun misrepresented its power. The air was cold and uncomfortable as Campbell rested in the prone position, half buried in the sand. Since first light, he had dozed off in spurts, only to awaken when his head nodded down to bury itself in his cover. The fear of discovery in the open desert choked him. The two AK-47s would provide little solace and even less protection should he be spotted by Iraqi soldiers in the vastness of the sand. There was no place to hide, nor to find cover or protection, unless he moved into the mountains east of him. To go that way would mean he would have to travel through the center of the Republican Guards. *I'll take my chances in the desert, at night.* He pulled more sand onto him, both for warmth and for camouflage.

As the day wore on, he observed little activity. The sounds of jet aircraft passed overhead from time to time but he couldn't see the sources of the sounds. A small group of men riding camels passed within a half-mile of his position in the late afternoon but he went unnoticed. There was no military traffic on the road only a mile distant. *Saddam Hussein sure doesn't seem to be fighting much of a war.*

Just before dusk, a small caravan of nomads passed down the road within view of his position. They were headed south. Campbell dreamed of joining them, disguised as a Bedouin, living the happy life of a gypsy until he reached the safety of Saudi Arabia where he could again join up with his unit. He thought of his childhood and the books he had read about the Middle East. *The Black Rose* came to mind. It had been one of his favorite adventure books when he was fourteen. The adventures of the hero in his search for the Black Rose seemed remote and romantic to Campbell now as he stared across the shimmering waves of light drifting skyward from the sand. He studied the brightly colored clothes of the women and the variety of cargo and animals in the caravan. *What a life. They probably don't give a damn who wins this war. I wonder if they even know there's a war going on? They probably think all this activity is just ol' 'So-Damn Insane' playing war games.* The caravan passed and his thoughts returned to the present.

Two or three more nights of walking, if my luck holds, and I'll be in Kuwait. Then what? The Republican Guard was supposed to be all over the northern Kuwaiti border. *Where the hell is the rest of the Iraqi army? Why haven't I seen anything? They have to be out there somewhere. They aren't <u>all</u> in Kuwait – are they?*

Shortly after the last rays of sunset faded into infinity, Campbell dusted off his captured weapons, checked the operation of the bolts and magazines, shouldered the rifles and resumed his march to the south.

He trudged through the sand, his thoughts as scattered as the winds of March, his attention unfocused and wandering. In the distance to his left, a range of mountains loomed black on the dark skyline. *I could travel by day in the mountains.* He shook his head. *Take too long. Couldn't travel at night.*

He stumbled on a small rock. *What the hell is that doin' out here in the middle of all this sand?* His heart jumped to his throat. *Mines! He sat and waited for a wave of trembling in his body to subside. Get a hold on yourself, Campbell. There's no logical reason to plant land mines here. You won't run into those for a while yet.*

He forced his mind to find another subject. It didn't have to search long. His stomach growled loudly and he looked down at his midsection. "Quit bitchin'. You've suffered through worse. We're both gonna get a lot hungrier before this is over, so you might as well get used to it," he said to his stomach.

He licked his dry lips and his thoughts became more immediate. His canteen was almost empty. He could stretch water as far as any man alive. He had grown up in the arid southwest, passed survival school with flying colors, and proven his desert fighting ability in peacetime exercises at Twenty-Nine Palms when he had been in the infantry. But the small amount of water and his current physical condition labored against him. *I hate to say it, stomach, but I've got a higher priority than you right now. Your hunger won't mean a damn thing if we don't get some water in the next day or so.*

Two hours into the night the smell of cooking food tantalized his nostrils. He lay on the soft ground and held his breath, listening for sounds. *What time do these people eat? It must be civilians. An army would eat before dark. Then again, who knows what the Iraqi army does?*

After several moments the faint sounds of voices reached his ears. Campbell followed the trail of sounds and smells to its source. A large sand dune between him and the camp had kept the sounds muffled. He crawled to the crest of the dune and peered into the group of people below. It was the caravan he had seen earlier in the day. A dozen or so tents grouped together in a rough circle dotted the landscape, highlighted by the flames of several small fires. The large fire in the center of the tents seemed to be the social center of activity.

His heartbeat quickened as he spotted the uniform of an Iraqi soldier on the outskirts of the rough circle of tents. He spotted two more near the large fire in the center. He hadn't noticed soldiers when he had seen the caravan earlier in the day. *How many? What kind of unit? Artillery? Infantry? Mechanized? Do they have sentries out?* He let his gaze wander the perimeter, but saw no sentries. *Maybe they're too far away from the fires to see. Maybe they know I'm here and they're encircling me right now.*

Stoney Livingston

Campbell moved closer, searching for sentries. He saw none. *This is really a squared-away outfit. Hell, with a marine rifle squad, I could walk in there and take 'em all out.*

The several small fires threw dancing light upon the surrounding tents. *This looks too easy. But what if it's really what it looks like and I pass up my chance for food and water?* Campbell was hungry and his need to replenish his water supply drove him closer. He moved next to a tent on the outer edge of the circle.

In the shadow of the outer tent he knelt and slowly lifted the bottom a few inches, searching for food or water. *I wish to hell they'd have these flaps rolled up. I could use the light from the fires. I wonder if any of the civilians are friendly? Snap out of it, Campbell. You can't take a chance. Besides, even if there are some friendlies, how are you going to pick them out? You just gonna walk up to 'em, one at a time, and ask until you find one that says he's friendly?* Inside there was darkness. He slipped into the tent and groped for anything that resembled food.

A carpet covered the sand inside the tent. *I'll bet it's one of those fancy Persian carpets.* He grinned at the irony. *They get a fortune for these things back home, and out here the gypsies throw them on top of dirt.*

At the sound of footsteps approaching the tent, Campbell felt his way quickly to a corner where he crouched behind a trunk. A soldier entered, his silhouette visible for a brief moment as he stepped into the tent. He sat on the edge of a cot. Campbell heard it creak in the darkness. The sound of rustling material caused Campbell's heart to race. *He's fishing for a match or a lighter. Christ, he'll be facing me when the lights come on.*

When the soldier struck the match and his attention was focused on the flame, Campbell smashed him in the face with the butt of his AK-47. The match dropped to the floor and extinguished as the soldier silently fell back, rolling from the edge of the cot to the carpet. Campbell pulled out his captured knife and slit the unconscious man's throat. He sheathed his knife and searched his victim's clothing, taking the matches first. From the dead man's wrist, he took a watch. It was a TAG Heuer. *I feel like scum taking a dead man's personal belongings but he sure as hell can't make use of it. I'll give it to Bob. He likes good watches. This guy must have been pretty well-off. Those watches aren't cheap.*

Campbell was breathing hard, concentrating on his search of the body, unaware that someone had entered the tent. Suddenly the newcomer stumbled into him in the darkness and fell loosely onto the body of the dead soldier. *Shit! Where the hell did he come from?*

Quickly Campbell lunged at the dark figure and grabbed an arm. Falling on top of the figure, he jammed his hand over its mouth. With his other hand, he jerked his knife free of its sheath and pressed the blade against the exposed throat. He hesitated for an instant. *A woman!* There was no mistaking the softness of her breasts against his arm as he held the knife to her throat.

"Don't move." He doubted she understood English but perhaps his tone of voice would be sufficient to persuade her to be still.

Her body went limp. Slowly he removed his hand from her lips, the knife still held tightly at her throat.

"You are an American?" she whispered. He felt her throat muscles move against the blade of his knife.

The soft English words startled Campbell. He was no longer wrestling with an Iraqi enemy. This woman could communicate with him. She might still be his enemy, but if she had to die it would not be out of ignorance but rather a choice she would make.

"You speak English?" he whispered.

"U.C.L.A., class of eighty-four." Her voice was low.

She sounded like any other average American. There was little or no accent. Campbell moved his knife from her throat. "I don't want to kill you, so don't make me."

"And I don't want to die."

"Then we agree on something."

"For the moment." Her breath was warm on his face. It carried with it the sweet smell of dates.

He became aware of her femininity. He lay on top of her, his face close to hers. With the knife in his hand on the ground next to her head, her breasts rubbed against his chest and he became self-conscious. He felt her body tremble against his. "I'm gonna get off you but please don't do anything stupid. I *will* kill you if I have to."

She nodded. "I understand."

Campbell stood slowly. Without thinking, he released her. He couldn't see her in the darkness and, for a short moment, fear bubbled into his throat. *Goddamn. That was stupid. "Here lies Jim Campbell. Killed because he was a stupid chauvinist." Christ, I didn't even search her.*

"I should light a candle. They are expecting it." Her voice calmed him. It gave away her location.

"Who are *'they'*?"

"My sister and her husband."

"Where are they?"

"Outside by the fire. This is their tent. They'll be here in a little bit."

"You sure speak good English."

"It was my major in college."

Campbell shook his head, a gesture lost in the darkness. "It's a small world."

She sat up slowly. "Smaller than most of us realize."

Campbell paused. "What was this soldier doing in here?"

"Probably looking for something to steal. It's not all that uncommon."

"How many of them are there out there?"

"You mean in our camp?"

"Yeah."

Desert Fire

"Four."

"That's all?"

"There's only one of you."

"That's enough for four of these guys." He nodded at the body.

"Three." She looked at the bloody body of the slain Iraqi soldier, her vision aided by the flame from the match as she lit a candle. A small shiver ran the length of her body, clearly noticeable in the flickering light of the candle.

Campbell remained motionless as she pursed her lips and blew out the match. "Who are you? What are you doing in the middle of the desert with your college degree? Why should I believe any of this crazy business?"

They studied each other in the flickering light. Campbell unconsciously ran his fingers through his hair and became aware of the matted blood. He thought of his bruised face. His flight suit was bloodied and torn, the survival knife still held in his hand. The AK-47 lay on the carpeted floor of the tent at his feet. His eyes searched her questioningly, wanting to believe she was on his side. *I'll have to kill you if you're not.* He sheathed the knife.

"I am Zahra Ramzi. My mother's family has lived here for hundreds of years. Whether you believe me or not is no concern of mine. And what I am doing here with my college degree is none of your business. Who are *you* and what are *you* doing here?"

Zahra was striking. Her dark hair hung to the middle of her back. A pair of large ebony eyes glowed from within the confines of perfectly spaced sockets, highlighted by long, thick eyelashes and eyebrows in the arc of a quarter moon. Her nose was rounded and slightly upturned. The desert sun had been kind to her skin. It showed none of the signs of leather yet. Campbell had seen lips shaped like hers only in drawings. They were the ones pictured on television commercials. They were the ultimate in femininity. *This isn't real. Those damn drugs. I know I'm hallucinating.*

"Uh. My name's Campbell – Jim Campbell. I'm a pilot."

"Well, Jim Campbell, it's nice to meet you." She held out her hand.

He hesitated.

"I like several of your American customs – shaking hands is one of them."

He took her hand in his and shook it briefly. For just a moment he forgot about the war. "I can't let the soldiers know I'm here." He released his grip on her hand.

"That's going to be difficult." She nodded to the dead man.

"I don't mean these guys in camp. I mean the rest of the Iraqi army. I've gotta find a way to take the rest of these guys out."

The sounds of voices nearing the tent sent Campbell to the carpeted sand in search of his weapons. He picked up an AK-47, stepped to the side of the entrance and whispered, "Back up. Give them room to get all the way in the tent. Don't say a word or they're dead."

Zahra stepped back two paces.

A man and woman stepped inside. Campbell slid in behind them and pushed them roughly toward Zahra.

"No! It is my sister."

Campbell stopped his advance.

Fear showed in the eyes of the man momentarily as they grew large. His face went blank and his fear was masked almost as quickly as it had shown. He spoke softly to Zahra.

Damn! How can anybody understand that shit? Campbell waved the barrel of his rifle. "English!" he whispered harshly.

With his eyes still focused on Campbell, the man spoke to Zahra in his native tongue.

"Silence," Campbell whispered, cutting the man off mid-sentence.

The man looked at the dead Iraqi soldier near Campbell.

Desert Fire

"Thees weel be deefecult to explain."

Campbell stood. "I don't really intend to do a lot of explainin'. Who are you?"

The man nodded. "Forgeeve me. I am Akbar Tahar. And thees is my wife, Tahaleh. Zahra is my wife's seester."

Campbell studied them. Tahaleh looked like a slightly older version of Zahra. The resemblance was unmistakable. "Does everybody speak English around here? I'm beginning to feel right at home."

Akbar said, "Many of us speak your language, but none as well as Zahra." He smiled proudly.

Akbar looked to be in his mid-to-late-thirties, though Campbell couldn't be sure. Beards have a way of hiding a man's true age. He appeared physically fit and able to cope with the hardships of daily life in the desert. The leathered skin on his face attested to many hours spent in the sun.

Campbell put Tahaleh's age at about thirty-one or two.

"I'll kill you all if I'm forced into it, English or no English."

Tahaleh stepped between the two men. "Have you not more important things to discuss?"

Akbar shot her a warning glance.

"He's an American; no doubt about it," said Zahra.

Akbar motioned to a pair of folding stools and the cot. "May we be seated?"

I oughta cut their throats, grab some food and water, and get the hell out of here. He waved the barrel of his rifle. "Go ahead. I'll stand."

Akbar and his wife sat on the cot, Zahra on one of the stools. Akbar waited until the women were seated. "You can not stay here. Eet ees too dangerous."

Campbell said, "No doubt about that. Have the soldiers got a vehicle?"

"Yes. It's parked on the east side of the tents."

"What kind is it?"

"I am not a military expert but it has large tires and it will carry several men."

"Personnel carrier. Does it have a machinegun mounted on it?"

Akbar nodded.

Campbell stared into the impassive face of his host. He tried to read him but had no success. "I have no guarantee you won't try to stop me. I'm going to have to tie you up. Is there anything in here I can use for rope?"

Akbar hesitated.

"Look, mister. I don't want to hurt you or any other civilians, but I intend to get back to Saudi Arabia alive. I either tie you up or I kill you deader'n hell. Which is it gonna be?" Campbell gripped the AK-47 tightly.

"We have rope," said Zahra.

"Wait," said Tahaleh. She stared at her husband. He returned her gaze for a moment then nodded.

"We are een seempathy with your cause," she said. "There is no need to tie us."

"What?" asked Campbell.

Akbar took over. "We want Saddam Hussein out of power. He has ruined our country. He weel bring Iraq to her knees eef he is allowed to leeve. It will not be needed to tie us up."

"I'm sure. Just like that, I'm supposed to forget about all of the religious crusades you people have espoused and the American flags you've burned, and all the fervor and hate you have for my country. Sorry, Mac, I'm not buyin' into that hand."

"Now, the choice ees yours, but even eef the camel faced the other way, I would tell you the same," said Akbar.

Campbell glanced at the two women. He faced Akbar. "I want to believe you, but I can't allow myself that luxury."

"My husband ees telling you truth. We want Saddam Hussein out of our country. I lose three brothers een the war weeth Iran, and my husband lose two. He have scars on chest from Iranian bombs. His mother and father killed by chemical weapons shoot by Iraq army. We have no wish to see him leeve to keel what ees left of our people."

"How many of your people out there are on our side?"

"Most. But some are not. They have beeg fear from reprisals," answered Akbar.

"Can you get messages to Saudi Arabia?"

Akbar nodded. "We have ways."

"Would you send a message to the Allies for me?"

"Eef eet helps to end war and remove Saddam Hussein, I weel deleever eet myself."

"Do you know what a SCUD missile is?"

Akbar nodded.

Campbell searched the faces of the Bedouins. Even if they were lying, he would still have the information and he would deliver it personally if he got back to friendly lines. It wouldn't hurt to take a chance. He thought of asking them to take him with them but his trust didn't go that far. He would have to sleep some time. He would be vulnerable.

"I can't stay here." He nodded to the body on the floor of the tent. "I can't let the other soldiers leave here alive. It's either me or them. After I give you the information I'm gonna try to take them out and use their vehicle for my escape. Can you tell me anything about positions south of here?"

"You weel need food and water," said Tahaleh. She turned to Zahra and continued to speak in English. "Get heem what food you can weethout getting attention."

Zahra stood and moved to the entrance.

Campbell made a move to stop her.

Akbar put his hand on Campbell's arm. Zahra stared at him. "You must trust us. She weel not put us in danger," said Akbar.

Campbell glanced from Zahra to Akbar. He looked back to the woman and nodded. "Okay."

Zahra left the tent quietly, her nose in the air.

Tahaleh rummaged through a small wooden chest. "We have food here for you but you should have a warm food before you go. Zahra weel bring warm food and water. I weel geeve to you other food." She began to pack dried meats and fruit into a burlap sack.

Campbell turned to Akbar. "You got a piece of paper?"

"What is your name?"

"Jim Campbell."

"I am happy to meet you, Mister Jeem Campbell."

CHAPTER 7

Campbell looked at the pieces of meat mixed with a brown rice. A coarse bread hung to the edge of the tin plate, covering a portion of the rice. His stomach growled as the fragrance from the steaming food hit his nostrils. He glanced up at Zahra, who held the plate out to him. "You wouldn't mind joining me for a bite of this, would you?"

Zahra picked up a portion of the mixture and put it in her mouth. As she chewed and swallowed with no hesitation, a smile danced in the corners of her eyes. When she finished, she said, "If it's poisoned then it looks like we'll die together." She hesitated, then smiled broadly. "Unless, of course, I took an antidote before I brought it in here."

Smart ass. "Real funny." He took the plate from her hand. "I'm not so sure whoever marries you is going to lead a very secure life." He wolfed down the food, using his hands for utensils, the softness of the warm rice welcomed by his eager stomach. Campbell looked at his hosts embarrassedly as his stomach pleaded loudly for more. "This stuff sure tastes better than what I've been getting. Thanks."

Akbar nodded silently.

Campbell's stomach was heavy, but satisfied. The strong cigarette provided to him by Akbar made him dizzy but it was a luxury to be enjoyed and savored. The meal was only ten minutes old in his stomach. He felt invigorated by the unfamiliar food and the excitement of what lay ahead. He was tired and sore and the food made him comfortably sleepy but anticipation overcame his physical weariness. His excitement was mixed with apprehension and deep fear of failure.

"You are very quiet, Jeem Campbell."

Campbell glanced at Akbar then took in the two women. He took a deep drag on the cigarette. "War is such a waste."

"Eet ees good for me to see that you do not enjoy doing what you do," said Akbar.

"That doesn't mean I can't do it better than Saddam's boys," defended Campbell.

Akbar shook his head. "I deed not mean that. Forgeeve me. I am certain you do your duties better than most men. I only mean eet ees good to see there ees hope for us all. When the soldiers who fight the war do not hate the people they fight, does that not mean we can someday be brothers?"

The muscles in Campbell's jaw tightened. "I don't know about all of that. I'm no one's brother. I don't have to be someone's brother just because I think war is a waste. You don't have to be related to a man to not want to see him killed."

"Maybe what I say ees lost een translation."

"Yeah. Maybe."

"Or maybe Jim Campbell doesn't wish to be related to a Bedouin."

Campbell looked at Zahra. The light from the candle danced on her face, highlighting her cheekbones. "Maybe it's you who's got a problem with mixed races, lady. Don't judge me by what *you* think *I* think."

Voices from outside the tent grew louder as the speakers called a name repeatedly.

"They are looking for heem." Akbar nodded at the body hidden under the cot.

Campbell rose to his feet and unsheathed the knife at his waist. He moved to the side of the tent door. When the soldier pushed his way into the tent, Campbell grabbed his head from behind, holding his hand over the man's mouth, and jabbed the knife under his ribs and into his kidney, twisting and wiggling the blade as it penetrated the man's organs. With no more than an exaggerated exhalation of breath, the man died on his feet. Campbell let the body gently to the carpeted floor.

He glanced at his three hosts. Akbar was impassive. Zahra and Tahaleh stood silently, fear written all over their faces – their whole bodies. "I'm sorry. I'll leave now. I didn't want to have to do that in here." He wiped the knife blade against his leg, sheathed it and picked up his AK-47s.

Zahra touched his arm at the door. "Forty miles south of here there are minefields if you stray more than twenty yards from the road."

His gaze met hers. "Thanks." He peeked outside the tent and moved stealthily into the night. He ran into another soldier as he rounded the corner of the nearest tent. With a single horizontal butt-stroke, he broke the man's neck with one of the AK-47s.

One left. Now if I can only take him out without firing a shot, I might make it out of here alive. He stepped over the dead soldier's crumpled body and continued towards the truck, his heart thumping in his ears.

The fourth soldier stood near the front of the truck, on the passenger side, smoking a cigarette casually as he gazed into the dark sky. The flames from the fires had burned low and gave little light at this distance. A brisk wind helped to hide the soft sounds of Campbell's footsteps as he approached at a casual walk. He was within ten yards of the unsuspecting soldier when the man turned and spotted him.

With his rifle already in his hands, the Iraqi soldier was able to fire, but he didn't. Maybe the uncertainty of what he saw caused him to hesitate. Campbell held no uncertainties. He fired a short burst into the man's chest and ran past him before the body hit the ground.

He fumbled for the ignition switch in the dark interior of the cab. Voices from the direction of the tents grew louder as the Bedouins approached the truck cautiously. *Where the hell is that ignition switch?* He slid across the seat and saw the crowd nearing the vehicle, the nearest man only twenty yards away. He fired a short burst into the air over their heads. They fell to the ground as one.

He shouted into the night. "If any of you speak English, you better tell the others not to move. I'm a crazy American and I'll kill the first person who comes another step in this direction."

The soft rumble of the Arabic language made its way through the ranks of those huddled on the ground. Someone spoke English. Campbell recognized the voice. "American. Go een peace. We do not weesh our women and children hurt. Leave us." It was Akbar.

Campbell pounded his fist on the truck's doorframe. "Sounds like a real good idea to me, mister. My only problem is a lack of keys. Tell your people to back away while I hot-wire this thing."

"That won't be necessary." It was Zahra's voice. "May I approach? I have the key."

"Put your hands high in the air an' walk this way real slow."

He watched her profile, dimly outlined by the smoldering fires of the camp behind her as she walked to him. When she was three feet from the door he ordered her to stop. He opened the door and put a foot on the ground. "Okay. You can lower your hands."

She dropped a key into his hand.

"Thanks. Maybe someday I'll pay you back," said Campbell.

"Don't thank me. My motives are selfish. I've seen how proficient you are at killing. Many of these people are my friends."

"Now that you've reduced this conversation to a business level, how'd you end up with the key?"

"The first man you killed. He was the driver. That's why they were searching for him. He had the key."

"Thanks anyway." He raised his voice. "All right, woman.

Desert Fire

Back away. Get back there with the rest of 'em."

He jumped back into the vehicle and pulled the door shut. In a few seconds he was on the road, the glow of the campfires disappearing from his view as he sped away from the Bedouin camp.

Campbell wondered how long it would be before the word got out that he was alive and headed south. *Damned truck sounds like Niagara Falls. I might as well transmit my location to their central command.*

With the Bedouin camp an hour behind him, it was time to abandon the truck. He pulled to the side of the road and turned the engine off. The silence of the desert almost choked him. His thoughts drifted to Zahra. *I'll bet she was queen of the campus when she was in college.*

He tried to picture her in American clothes, driving a Ford or Plymouth. He couldn't complete the picture. He tried it without clothes. He didn't have much luck there either. *I'm losing it. What the hell did they do to my mind?*

The radio crackled. Campbell jumped at the unexpected sound. He listened to the unfamiliar language. The speaker finished his transmission and the radio squelched out.

Who the hell was he talking to? I must be close. These radios don't have much range.

The sound of a motorized vehicle approaching sent his heart to his throat. He jumped from the cab of the truck and up to the machinegun mounted behind the driver, in the front of the troop area. He cocked the gun and ducked back into the truck bed. *What if they've got night scopes?* His heart beat like thunder in his ears.

The enemy vehicle was closer. Campbell couldn't see it but he knew, from the sound, it was a personnel carrier like the one he drove. *How many soldiers? What are they doing out here at this hour? Maybe I should run. No, if they've got night scopes, I'd be dead meat.*

Stoney Livingston

The approaching vehicle stopped only thirty yards away. Campbell sat with his back to the rear of the cab, clutching an AK-47, his palms wet and slippery with sweat, his muscles wound to the point of snapping. The clanking sounds of men debarking the vehicle pushed him to the edge of panic but he held on. One of the men said something quietly. A second voice answered at a normal conversational level.

They think it's abandoned.

A flashlight beam cut across the top of the truck. *It's over. They're gonna find me, like a rat backed into a corner.* The beam worked its way to the back of the truck. Campbell saw the head of the flashlight come into view. He fired a short burst. The light tumbled to the ground.

Campbell dropped his AK-47 and jumped to the heavy machinegun. He swung the barrel in an arc and fired on the Iraqi vehicle. The heavy slugs bored into the cab of the dark shadow before him. A door flew open and the body of the driver fell to the sand. Campbell released the trigger on the machinegun and picked up his AK-47. He jumped to the ground and skirted the passenger side of his vehicle. A third soldier crouched low ten yards to his front. Campbell pulled the trigger and held it. The man's body arched and jerked violently then crashed to the ground. Campbell released the trigger and charged the Iraqi personnel carrier.

It was over. There had been only three men in the truck. Campbell found a night scope in the battered personnel carrier but it was no use to him. A heavy caliber slug had smashed it beyond repair.

The radio crackled to life. The urgency in the voice on the radio told him what he didn't want to hear. The Iraqis had, at the very least, notified someone they had found an unattended personnel carrier; at the most, they had been able to report enemy contact. He was now in a running battle with the Iraqi Army.

He ran to his confiscated personnel carrier, threw his rifle into the cab and jumped behind the wheel. The engine roared to life and he made a skidding U-turn. He held the throttle wide open for ten minutes then turned sharply to his left and entered the minefield.

If I'm not blown to hell, this should work. It's my only chance.

He drove almost half a mile, his head wanting to burst with every beat of his heart. He knew he was in a minefield. *Where the hell are all the mines?* He stopped the truck on top of a large dune. *Goddamn, I could sure use a cigarette.* He exited the truck carefully, probing the ground with his knife before he put his feet onto the sand. When he had checked the area thoroughly at his feet, he lay prone and searched the sand on the downward slope of the dune, inching forward as he probed with his knife.

Near the bottom of the dune his knife struck the edge of a solid object. He probed carefully, tracing the outline of the buried article until his knife had described a circle eighteen inches in diameter in the sand. *There really are goddamn mines out here! Jesus! This thing's big enough to take out a battleship!* He removed the magazine from the AK-47 on his back and stuck the rifle, barrel-first, into the sand in front of the mine. Carefully, he retraced his path to the truck at the top of the dune.

Inside the cab he picked up his canteen. It was empty. A stray bullet had struck it in the center, exploding it outward. Campbell tossed it to the floor of the cab. *I should have taken enough time to search that other vehicle. Oh well, that only makes this little show that much more believable.* He grabbed the remaining AK-47 and the small bag containing the food the Bedouins had prepared for him and stepped gingerly into the sand. With his right hand, he released the truck's emergency brake and held his breath as it started to roll slowly.

He wanted to watch it all the way to the mine but prudence dictated a safer position. He scrambled to the lee side of the dune, careful to stay in the tracks left by his vehicle. He had barely crested the dune when the truck struck the mine. The sand shifted below him and the night sky turned white for an instant. The sound of the explosion was deafening. Pieces of the ill-fated truck buzzed into the night sky as sand rained down on him like a summer downpour of rain.

Campbell brushed away the sand and reached forward with his knife, probing for mines as he inched his way north. He brushed the sand behind him as he moved, obliterating evidence of his passage. It was slow going but it was his only hope. If his calculations were correct, the northern end of the minefield was less than two miles from his position, give or take a mile.

Campbell lay buried in the sand, only the top of his head and his eyes exposed as he watched the soldiers on the road. They were lined up, staring at the wreckage of his APC He was tempted to emerge from the sand and fire upon them. They were lined up like ducks in a shooting gallery, but there were too many. An Iraqi helicopter flew overhead, buzzing the wreckage of the truck.

He had made only seven hundred yards before daylight had forced him to dig in. The discovery of four mines in his path had added to his caution and slowed him considerably as the night had progressed.

His mouth was dry and his muscles weary as he contemplated first the long day ahead, then the nerve-wracking search for mines as he probed further north with the coming of darkness. Then, there were always the Iraqi soldiers. He estimated their number at twenty. There were five APCs. He felt the bag of rations below him. *I'll never make it without water. If I surrendered, at least I'd get some water. Maybe even have a chance to make another break.* He remembered his treatment at the hands of his captors. *I don't think that's such a good idea. The beatings were bad but I can't handle the drugs. I'd rather die out here.*

Desert Fire

The helicopter made a last pass over the wreckage, hovered above it a moment, then disappeared to the south. Campbell watched apprehensively as the soldiers mounted their vehicles and left slowly in the same direction. He buried his face in the sand and cried silently. He cried with relief and he cried for the hopelessness of his situation; for information he wanted desperately to get to the Allied Forces, and the things he wanted to do with his life. *If it all ends here, my life has been wasted.* He thought of his childhood and then flight school. He thought of Bob Wyman. A smile creased his face. *Not all wasted, I guess.*

CHAPTER 8

Zahra Ramzi stood to the side of the crowd of men as they gathered around the Iraqi truck and listened to the driver's tale of the enemy soldier killed in the minefield in the early morning hours. Zahra knew it was the American pilot. She felt a momentary loss as she stared into the sunset, her eyes searching the dunes to the south. The war with Iran had taken her childhood sweetheart, Jousef, and now the American Jim Campbell.

The caravan had traveled quickly during the day and much ground had been covered. The vast minefields lay only a mile south of where they were camped. If only she had told him she was an American agent.

She looked at the soldier and stifled the desire to cry out and tell him what a fool he was. What fools they all were. Saddam Hussein was a madman, a butcher. This war could not be won. This war was not a righteous one. Let the Kuwaiti people live in peace. What had so many deaths gained Iraq over the years? Were the people richer? Wiser? More respected? Better fed and clothed? Was their education greater?

She thought again of Campbell – an educated man. His knowledge gone with the passing of his soul. *What a waste. What a waste for all of the lost souls.*

The soldier told of how Campbell had encountered one of their personnel carriers and, after a short battle, had turned north and into the minefield, and how he had been blown into nothingness by a large mine only a few miles south of where the caravan camped.

Zahra shuddered at the thought of his death – any death. There was too much death in the Middle East – and almost always it was violent. She wanted to find the wreckage and see for herself that Campbell was dead but knew it was a foolish wish. Land mines respected no nationality. Perhaps when the war was over and the mines cleared, she would go to the spot and say a prayer for him.

Though not deeply religious, Zahra held strong views of her own about God and spirit – views not necessarily in compliance with those of her kinsmen. Perhaps her beliefs had been influenced by her American friends and her love of their way of life. Life was so precious to Americans. They attached so much importance to a single life that even her sister, Tahaleh, could not understand.

There were many bad Americans, to be sure, but there were many more who were good. Their United States Constitution was a document revered by Zahra.

Akbar's touch on her arm brought her out of her reverie. "Have you seen Tahaleh?"

Zahra shook her head. "Not for almost an hour. She was going to visit with your mother. Perhaps she is still talking to her."

Akbar shook his head. "I checked. She is not there."

Zahra smiled. "You worry too much. You know she likes to take long walks with her dog." She nodded to the soldiers. "Her greatest danger is from the soldiers, and they are too busy boasting to bother with women right now."

Akbar followed her nod and spat. "Dogs! They have all of the power now but the day will come when the winds blow fortune another direction."

Zahra looked into the eyes of her brother-in-law. "I hope we all live long enough to see that day, Brother."

Akbar returned her gaze. "If not, we will die knowing that it will happen and that we played a part."

Zahra looked to the south. "But how many more will die?"

Akbar put his hand on her shoulder. "It is sad what happened to the American. I think he was a good man. He was strong and intelligent. But Allah was against him. The odds were too great. You felt an attraction for this man, didn't you?"

Zahra shrugged his hand from her shoulder. "No more than any other member of the resistance."

Akbar smiled sadly. "It is true then. You were attracted to him. Perhaps you are more American than you are Arab. I saw nothing in him that would appeal to an Arab woman."

Zahra faced him. "How can you speak for Arab women? How can you speak for any women? You are not female. What gives you the right to say those kinds of things?"

Akbar studied the sand at his feet. "Perhaps he reminded you of someone at the American University. Someone who was kind to you."

Zahra scowled at him. "He reminded me of no one. He was only who he was." She looked again to the south. "And now he is nothing more than another death to add to the list of dead."

Akbar looked into her face. "I will leave you to your thoughts. This man has troubled you more than I thought. I guess you are right. I know nothing of how a woman thinks. I will look for Tahaleh now. If you wish, we will talk after the evening meal."

Zahra's voice softened. "Thank you, Akbar. I know you are trying to help. Tell Tahaleh I will help her shortly."

Dusk was almost night when Akbar turned to leave. Zahra watched him go, silently, her mind racing to rationalize the loss she felt at Campbell's death. *He was a human. It is always sad when a human life is taken prematurely.* She knew she kidded only herself. Campbell had been special. Why he had been special, she didn't know. She only knew he had been.

She thought of Yousef and the years they had spent together in school, his dreams of becoming a teacher and educating every child in the Middle East. She remembered the day he had left for the war with Iran. He strutted proudly before her in his new uniform, pledging his love and devotion to her and promising to bring Iran to her knees single-handedly so that he could get on with the business of teaching. Yousef was only twenty years old when he died on the front line two weeks after his departure.

Zahra had cried a lot. She cried until her throat and stomach hurt and she could no longer see through her swollen eyes. She cried until she thought she would die of grief. Tahaleh had saved her from herself. Her older sister had hugged her and cried with her until Zahra could no longer stand the pain she was inflicting upon others.

She thought of Tahaleh now and found it odd that she had been missing from camp so long. With the coming of darkness she was always at Akbars' side. Zahra hurried to their tent.

Akbar stood just outside the door of the tent, the worried look on his face emphasized by the light from the large fire in the center of the circle of tents. The deep shadows on his brow told Zahra of the furrows caused by his concern. "Tahaleh hasn't shown up yet?" she asked.

Akbar shook his head. "Something is wrong. I will get some of the men and we will search for her."

"I will go with you."

Akbar shook his head. "No, you should stay and prepare the meal. She will be hungry when we find her."

Something rubbed against Zahra's leg. "Her dog!" She turned to see Tahaleh puffing towards them at a brisk walk. "Tahaleh. Where have you been?" said Zahra, a scolding note in her voice.

Tahaleh walked past them, into the tent. "Come," she said as she entered.

Quickly Akbar and Zahra stepped into the tent.

Tahaleh sat on a stool.

"What is it? Where have you been? Are you all right?" asked Akbar.

Tahaleh nodded, still drawing deep breaths. Akbar and

Zahra remained standing near the door flap. "I have found the American," she said excitedly. "He is alive."

Zahra felt her heart beat wildly in her chest. "Alive? Where is he?"

Tahaleh pointed to the west wall of the tent. "Not far. Less than a kilometer. He needs help. I gave him what water I had with me but he has been bitten in the neck by a scorpion. The area is badly inflamed and his physical condition is not good for fighting off the poison. He might die."

Zahra gathered up supplies even as she spoke. "Was he injured by the land mine?"

Tahaleh shook her head. "I don't think so but he is very weak and very sick. He hasn't touched any of the food we gave him."

"Where is he? I'm going to him," said Zahra.

"Have the soldiers left camp yet?" asked Akbar.

"I don't care. The man needs help."

"He is two fingers east from south, about three-quarters of a kilometer," said Taheleh. "He is buried in the sand. Only his face is visible."

Zahra lifted the tent flap. "I have water and medicines. I will be back shortly if I need help."

"Zahra. The soldiers," said Akbar.

"I will watch for them. Don't worry." She entered the darkness outside.

It took only a few moments for her to find Tahaleh's trail in the sand and, even without the aid of the moon to guide her, she was able to follow it by feeling the indentations left by her sister's feet. It was an old Arab trick. The Arabs say even a blind man can track his quarry in the desert.

Zahra hurried carelessly across the dunes. She hoped the minefields were where they were supposed to be. In several minutes she almost fell over Campbell's supine form as she stepped up her pace. She fell to her knees next to him, placed the bag containing the salves and medicines nearby, and brushed the sand from Campbell's covered upper chest and neck.

"Can you hear me?"

Campbell groaned softly. His eyes were closed.

He is almost dead. I'm too late. She felt his neck for a pulse. It was weak but it was still detectable.

The sound of cloth swishing in the darkness only a few feet behind her caused her to turn with a start. One of the soldiers from their camp stood three feet from her. "Why are you sneaking up on me like that?" The Arabic flowed from her lips like fire.

The soldier was not intimidated. "What are you doing out here? And who is that man?"

With one hand partially hidden from the soldier's view, she brushed sand over the exposed part of Campbell's flight suit. "I am tending to my sick brother. He is a deaf mute and he is very ill. Sometimes he makes strange noises that frighten the others in camp."

"Why is he buried in the sand?"

"It is part of the treatment."

"Part of what kind of treatment? I have never heard of such a treatment."

Zahra was frantic. She couldn't think of answers all night. "Our father was a healer. In the old days, when all else seemed to fail, the sick were partially buried in the sand to draw strength from the earth." She looked quickly at Campbell, who remained motionless.

"He looks dead to me. Why don't you just cover him where he is and let him rot? He won't smell any different than the live ones." The soldier laughed at his own joke.

"Leave us in peace. Can't you see he is dying?"

"If he's dying then he won't care if you and I carry on the act of living, will he?"

Zahra felt the bile of fear in her throat. The soldier grabbed her by the arm and threw her backwards into the sand. He spat on Campbell's body and quickly faced her. "A man needs a woman from time to time, and out here there are not many women. You are pretty for a Bedouin slut. I'll say you've left many a man smiling from the look of you."

Zahra back-peddled a few yards, drawing the soldier and his attention from Campbell. Her legs were exposed to the middle of her thighs by her actions. She pulled her heavy dress quickly to her ankles and covered her face. "Please. Don't do this. We have done nothing to you."

The soldier glanced quickly at Campbell's unmoving form. He faced her and smiled, his lips twisted and curled. "Too bad your brother cannot see his sister give her flower to a real man." He took a step in her direction.

Zahra knew she was no physical match for the soldier. He would win and have his way with her. If she resisted, he would beat her. She needed her health to complete her mission. "Please. No."

The soldier's voice softened. "Don't fight it. There is no one here to help you. We can do this right and it will feel good for both of us. Or you can fight it and I will screw a corpse."

A shudder ran the length of her body. She couldn't let herself give in to this man. "No!" She tried to stand but he was too close. His big hand struck her full in the face, knocking her to her back.

He stood over her, breathing heavily. "How do you want it, Bitch?"

"Kill me."

He stepped back. "You think highly of what you have between your legs. It's no different than any other woman's." He cocked the rifle and pointed it to her head. "It makes no difference to me. Your body will be warm enough to satisfy my needs."

Zahra closed her eyes and waited for the end. Her heart pounded so hard against her chest she knew it would explode before the bullet took her life. The sound of the soldier's pant legs

114

swishing as he walked brought her eyes open quickly. He pointed the rifle at Campbell's head. "No!" She shouted.

He turned and faced her. "What about it? His life for my pleasure?"

Zahra's heart seemed to stop beating. "Please. Don't shoot him."

He moved back to her. "You haven't answered my question, Bitch."

"Yes."

"What? I didn't hear you. Beg for his life. Let me hear you beg for him."

Tears flowed down her cheeks. "Please don't kill him. I will do whatever you want me to do."

He squatted next to her, his unshaven face only inches away. His lips curled in a cynical grin. He reached out gently and touched her face. "That's much better my little Bedouin whore."

She recoiled at his touch.

"No, that will never do. You must beg me to touch you."

Zahra looked at Campbell's dark form only a few feet away. Her eyes rotated back to the soldier. "Please touch me."

He put his rifle in the sand next to him and lifted her dress. Zahra's skin crawled as his hand moved up her calf and onto her thigh. He groaned and made a small convulsive movement. "Talk to me some more. Tell me how badly you want me to touch you." His hand touched her crotch. She shuddered. The soldier misread her reaction to his touch. "You see? I knew you were hot-blooded when I first saw you. Tell me how good it feels."

She closed her eyes. "It feels good."

"Do you want more?"

"Yes, I want more."

He pulled his hand from between her legs. "Get undressed. I want to see you completely naked. Do it now!"

He remained kneeling as she unwrapped her dress and removed her veil. She stood naked in the cool night air, goose bumps of fear and cold covering her body. The soldier spread her clothing on the sand, his face inches away from her crotch. He kept his eyes glued there. When he had the clothes spread to his satisfaction, he said, "Lay on your back, woman. I'm sure I don't have to tell *you* what to do. If you're as good as you look, I may want more than one round. And you better make it good. Do you understand?" He jerked his head in Campbell's direction.

"Yes. Yes, I understand." She sat on her clothes and glanced at his rifle. It was too far away. Desperately she grasped for hope that she would find a way to stop him.

"I said on your back woman!"

She fell back and lay unmoving, her legs tightly drawn together.

"If I have to tell you what to do, I might as well kill your brother now. You aren't convincing me, do you hear?"

Slowly she spread her legs. Fully clothed, he moved over her and kissed her breasts, first one, then the other. He bit them viciously and tore at her pubic hair as he tried to force his fingers into her body. She convulsed with pain and his excitement grew to a frenzy. He jumped back and undid his trousers. As they fell to his knees, he was on her, jabbing at her with his erection. She squirmed and wiggled away several times just as he was about to enter her. In his excitement, he appeared to take her movements as signs that she was as excited as he.

"I knew it. It's good, isn't it? So good. Oooh. Ooh Settle down, you hot-blooded little bitch."

A button on his uniform shirt cut her chest and she jumped with pain.

"That's it! It *is* good. Oh, yes. Oh yes. Oh..."

An explosion near her face ripped the night air. There was a bright orange-white flash and the soldier's head snapped abruptly to one side. Pieces of meat and bone showered her head and upper body. He fell limply on top of her and she felt a warm fluid oozing between her breasts and around her neck on its way to the clothes beneath her.

Her ears still rang from the blast as she pushed the soldier's body from her and rolled to her side. Campbell lay in the prone position holding the dead man's rifle shakily supported with arms supported by his elbows in the sand. The barrel wavered over her.

"I'm sorry. Did I get to him in time?"

Zahra felt the rush of her emotions. She was oblivious to the blood and brains on her bare flesh. "Yes."

"Good." He dropped the rifle and fainted.

Another kind of fear gripped Zahra as Campbell fell face down in the sand. She reached out and drew him to her, wrapping her naked body around his flight suit and hugging him tightly. She knew she should see to his injury but her body trembled uncontrollably. It was all she could do to hold onto him tightly and tremble as the silent tears from her eyes washed the sand from both of their faces. Soon she sobbed unashamedly and convulsively, her body jerking spasmodically with each deep breath until sleep overcame her.

"Praise Allah. Are you all right?"

Zahra pulled her face out of Campbell's dirty, matted hair and looked into Akbar's face. The sky told her it was after midnight.

"Zahra. Are you all right?" repeated Akbar. He covered them both with a blanket.

"Yes, I'm all right."

Akbar looked at the body of the soldier. "Did he... Was he able to…"

"No, Akbar, my dear brother. The American killed him before he was successful."

Akbar breathed a sigh of relief. "And what of the American? Is he still alive?"

Zahra's heartbeat quickened. She wet her lips with her

tongue and held them close to Campbell's mouth and nose. She felt his warm breath against her lips and said, "Yes. He's still alive. Can you help me get him back to camp? He needs cleaned and bathed and tended. His body is full of fleas and he is dehydrated. If he has lived this long since he was stung, the scorpion won't kill him, but a combination of other things might." She got to her feet shakily and wrapped the blanket around her.

"I will carry him back to camp," said Akbar. "But first we must hide the body of the soldier.

Zahra looked at the grotesque form lying in the sand atop her discarded clothing. The trousers around his ankles brought back her struggle vividly. The left side of his head was a caved-in mass of goo. Drying, semi-liquid brain clung to the destroyed head and face where it had stopped flowing sometime during the night. "Leave him for the desert."

"We can't do that, Zahra. We must hide him from the others."

"A burial is too good for him."

"That is unlike you, my sister."

"I'm sorry, Akbar. You are right. It's just that..." The tears began to fall again.

Akbar put his arm around her and said, "I will help get the American back to camp, then I will take care of the soldier. Come. Let us go."

Akbar carried Campbell with little help from her, and only one short rest break, the distance to camp. He deposited the American on Zahra's cot and left quickly to take care of the soldier's body.

Zahra sat next to the cot, clad only in the blanket provided her by Akbar. Tahaleh fussed busily about the tent, readying a pan of warm water and liniments. The dim glow of a single candle lighted the inside of the tent.

"He is very near death, Zahra. Perhaps we risk too much by keeping him here. There are those in camp who would turn him in and us along with him. We will never be able to keep him hidden when we move."

Zahra continued to stare at Campbell's face, shadows cast by the flickering candle dancing all about it. "Then I will stay with him, Tahaleh."

Tahaleh placed the pan of warm water next to the cot. "What happened out there tonight? Why are you wrapped in a blanket? It isn't that cold tonight."

Zahra told her sister the story of the soldier and how Campbell had shot him just before he was able to carry through with his act of rape. Tahaleh undressed Campbell and bathed him as Zahra haltingly told the story.

"...and he said, 'good.' Then he passed out."

Tahaleh was wiping Campbell's chest with a wet cloth. She halted her motions and looked into Zahra's face. "I don't think this man has the strength to roll over, much less do as you have said. See here?" She pointed to a large red mark, centered at the base of his neck. It was irregularly shaped and extended from his ear to the bottom of his shoulder blade. "It burns like fire. His fever is so high I doubt he could comprehend anything enough to know right from wrong. If he were conscious, he would be delirious."

That is just like Tahaleh, thought Zahra. *She has outwardly dismissed my ordeal to discuss the feasibility of the American's ability to react to the situation. But I know her. And I know she is crying inside. She tries to be so logical but she fools no one.* Zahra shrugged. "I only know what he did, not what he is capable or incapable of doing."

Tahaleh put a cool moist cloth to Campbell's neck. He moaned and moved restlessly for a moment. "Wash his hair while I put an ointment on his neck," said Tahaleh.

Zahra took the cloth from her sister's hand. "I'm sorry, Tahaleh. I should have been helping. I guess I just had to talk first."

Tahaleh looked at her then leaned over and embraced her

tightly. "Oh, my little sister. I hurt for you. You needn't tell me you are sorry. It is I who am sorry. I should have gone with you."

Tears flowed down both women's cheeks. Zahra said, "No. Never think that. Nothing happened. Everything is fine. Don't blame yourself."

Campbell stirred. The two broke their embrace and looked down at him. His eyes were open. He seemed to be trying to focus on Zahra. His lips moved slowly and Zahra put her ear next to his mouth.

"I can see you in a Plymouth now," he said.

"What do you mean?" Asked Zahra.

Campbell was unconscious again.

"What did he mean by that?" asked Tahaleh.

"I don't know."

"What is this 'Plymouth' he sees you in?"

"There is an American car called a Plymouth, but that makes no sense."

"Perhaps he will tell us when he gets better."

"He's probably delirious, like you said."

Tahaleh looked at Campbell, lying motionless on the cot. "No doubt."

CHAPTER 9

The odor of cooking food reached into Campbell's brain. He opened his eyes slowly and looked up at the ceiling of the tent. The flaps were rolled down and, with the exception of one small, screened window and the door, little light made its way into the interior. His mouth salivated and his stomach growled loudly. He licked his cracked lips and winced.

A woman stood over him. It wasn't the Ramzi woman but her older sister. *What was her name?* "Hi."

She jumped at his spoken word. "I deed not know you awake."

Campbell smiled. He felt the cracks in his lips deepen and begin to bleed. "Chow sure smells good. What's cookin'?"

She smiled. The room seemed to lighten up a bit. "You are hungry?"

"A little – if you have it to spare." He closed his eyes. *Tahaleh. That's it.* "I guess I didn't thank you properly the last time you gave me food, Tahaleh."

"You remember my name? Oh, you are much better than I thought."

"I could hardly forget the name of a woman as beautiful as you. If Akbar wasn't such a good guy, I'd probably be chasing after you right now." *Might as well hit her with all of the names. Let her know I'm not as down and out as she might think.* "And your sister Zahra – I hope I'm pronouncing it right – I still owe her a favor for bringing me the key to that truck as fast as she did."

"It is good to see you have memory not affected by your problems in desert."

Campbell twisted his head for a better view of the interior of the tent. "I don't remember coming all the way back up here. As a matter-of-fact, to tell the truth, I don't see how it's possible. I must have been out of it a lot longer than I thought." That worried him.

Tahaleh laughed. "We are south of where you last see us. Maybe forty or fifty kilometers."

Panic shot through him. *The Iraqi army!* He tried to sit up but dizziness overcame him and he fell back onto the cot. "Where's my rifle?" He felt the rough blanket against his skin. "Where are my clothes?"

"Be still. You wait. Zahra explain everything. Better English. Still too weak."

"Where is she? I need some explaining real fast."

"I'm right here, Captain Campbell."

He twisted his head to face the door. Zahra held a steaming bowl in her hands. She placed it on a small stool nearby and sat carefully next to him on the cot.

"Quit calling me 'Captain Campbell'. My name is Jim for crying out loud."

She smiled. "You still seem to like to give the orders."

Her smile was even brighter than her sister's. He thought he detected a change in her attitude towards him, a warming. "Sorry. I just prefer Jim. I'm a fighter pilot. If I could do it as a civilian, I would, but there just isn't a big demand for civilian fighter pilots. Everyone in the military has to have a rank. It's their rules, not mine."

"Are you hungry? Do you feel like eating?"

"If you can spare the food, I could use a bite but, first, I want my rifle and my knife." He paused. "And even more importantly, I want my clothes."

Zahra giggled.

"Did I say something funny?"

"You Americans are funny people. And you are funny even

for an American."

"You think it's funny that I want my clothes?"

"I think it's funny that you think of them as more important than food, or even weapons."

Campbell pulled the blanket a little tighter around his neck. "So, did Akbar have a lot of trouble undressing me?"

Zahra laughed a bubbly laugh. "Don't fish, Captain…Jim." Her voice softened when she said his name. "Tahaleh undressed you. I would have done it myself but I was a little tired and weak at the time."

Campbell felt the heat rise to his ears. He looked at Tahaleh, standing quietly behind her younger sister, then back to Zahra. "Can you tell me why everything seems so funny to you today?"

The smile in her eyes faded and was replaced by a faraway look. "After last night, I am happy to be alive. Give me a few days and I will become more somber if that will make you happy."

He looked to Tahaleh for help. She said nothing. "What happened last night?"

Zahra looked intensely at him. "You don't remember?"

Campbell closed his eyes tightly and concentrated – nothing but shades of blurred grey. He opened them. "Did the soldiers find out I'm still alive?"

He thought he detected a brief flash of disappointment in her expression.

"No. There was a little trouble but you were not the cause."

Campbell breathed a sigh of relief. "That's good to know. Can I have my clothes now?"

Zahra nodded to Tahaleh who picked up a maroon bundle and placed it on the cot at his feet.

"What's that? Where's my flight suit?"

"Akbar used it to cook this stew. Would you like some?" She picked up the bowl.

"He *burned* it? Are you people crazy? If I'm captured,

these ragheads – no offense – will shoot me as a spy."

Zahra picked up the bowl and dished out a large spoonful. "I don't really think it matters what you are wearing if they catch you," she said with a light-hearted smile. "You would welcome a bullet."

"Do you find that amusing?"

She straightened out her smile with obvious difficulty. "No. I don't find that amusing." Her smile returned. "But they will not catch you."

"That's nice to know. Can you make me invisible or something?"

"An idea came to me last night and I think you'll agree it's a good one." She put the spoon against his lips gently.

Campbell slurped the warm soup down. His stomach growled. "So tell me."

"You are my brother."

"Good. I really like that one. I'm sure everybody will believe that. I believe it. See how easy it is to convince people?" He looked at Tahaleh. "Do you believe I'm your brother?"

She nodded.

"With your dark hair, you could pass as an Arab."

"Until they ask me a question."

"You are a deaf mute."

Campbell paused. "Not bad. But what about papers?"

"Akbar is taking care of that right now."

"That Akbar is a regular miracle worker, isn't he?"

Zahra grinned. "Don't you see? It's perfect. Even those in camp – with only a few exceptions – won't know who you really are. And those few exceptions are trusted members of the resistance."

"How did I get here? And what's my name?"

"You arrived late last night by car. Our cousin drove you. You have been very ill and there is no one at home to take care of you. This will explain why you are bedridden. Your name is

Ahmed"

"Ahmed?" He paused. "Okay, I'm Ahmed. Which way are you going when you leave? And how soon before that happens?"

"We are staying here for two more days, then we return to Baghdad."

"Baghdad? No thanks. If I'm going to Baghdad, I'm landing at their airport in an F-18." He took another spoonful of soup. "Why are you going back to Baghdad?"

"This is the end of the line for us. We make contact with our agent and exchange information."

"How do you people make a living?"

"We buy and sell things. We buy in the north and sell in the south and vice-versa. In the States, we would be like those people who go to flea markets and swap meets and yard sales. We buy low and sell high."

"What are you going to buy around here?"

Zahra clucked. "Too many questions. Eat your soup."

Campbell kept his eyes on Zahra's face as she fed him. He knew she was aware of his gaze but he ignored the self-consciousness that any other time would have made him avert his gaze.

When he finished the soup Zahra placed the bowl on the stool. Campbell said, "You are one pretty woman, you know that?" He saw the blood rush to her face. "I didn't mean anything by that other than what I said. It's a statement of fact. That's all – you know – just an observation."

Her olive complexion regained control. "Thank you, Captain. It is nice to know you find me pretty. I wonder how I would compare if we were at UCLA?" She said it warmly, almost objectively.

Campbell smiled, the pain causing him to twitch. "Favorably, I'd say. Real favorably. And you called me 'Captain' again." He was comfortable, both with his new identity and his new relationship with Zahra. She appeared genuinely friendly and she seemed happy about something.

"You are quick. I'll give you that. I'll bet you have a pretty blonde wife or girlfriend back home," she said.

"No wife. Several women who I consider friends. And not all of 'em are blondes."

She laughed. The world was a brighter place for Campbell as he watched her. "At least you are honest. And I believe you."

"I could be bragging."

"Somehow I don't think you are."

"I feel like I know a lot more about you than I can remember. That's weird, I know, 'cause we've only met once before...but . . .Oh well, maybe I'm confusing you with a pretty spy I read about in a book."

Zahra cast a nervous glance at her sister.

Akbar burst into the tent.

Tahaleh spoke to him rapidly. Akbar answered solemnly. Campbell didn't have to understand the words to know that something was very wrong. He waited patiently for Akbar and Tahaleh to finish their lengthy exchange.

Campbell looked at Zahra. The happiness was gone from her face. "What's wrong?" he said.

"Everything."

"Could you be a little more specific?"

"Our contact has been compromised. Even as we speak, the army is hunting him. We can't pass our information to the coalition nations."

"Isn't there some other way?" Campbell felt his heartbeat increase. A hollow feeling grew, low in his chest.

Akbar said, "I think we weel not get the information to your countrymen until they lose many planes to kill the SCUD missile launchers that not SCUD missile launchers."

"Decoys. Or dummies," said Campbell.

"Yes, that too."

Campbell shook his head.

Desert Fire

"That isn't the worst," said Zahra.

"He couldn't get my papers?"

"The army has large stores of chemical weapons within range of the southern Kuwaiti border. If the coalition forces advance, Saddam Hussein has ordered his troops to use them."

Campbell tried to sit up. "Where are they? I've gotta get out of here." He fell back.

Zahra leaned over him and scolded. "Don't be foolish. There is nothing you can do until you have your strength back. It isn't necessary to be the macho American right now."

Campbell looked up at her. He resented what she said and he resented her. The closeness he had felt only moments ago was gone. For about the flicker of a flashbulb he hated all Arabs. "Go to hell, lady. The men in my unit attack SCUD sites. If I have a breath in my body, none of 'em are gonna get killed trying to take out dummy SCUDs protected by anti-aircraft batteries." He sat up, holding the blanket to his waist, trembling from a mixture of rage and physical weakness.

Akbar put his hand on Campbell's shoulder. "It is not necessary, Captain Jim. I know you mean your words. Women do not understand."

A rush of kinship with the Arab man washed through Campbell. He wanted to cry but could not. He was ashamed of his reaction to Zahra's remark. Akbar was right. She wasn't indicative of all Arabs. She was foremost a woman and he could see an American woman responding in the same way. He looked up at Zahra. What he felt must have shown.

"I don't know why I said that. I'm sorry," she said.

"If you knew what I've been thinking, you wouldn't be, so I guess that makes us both sorry." He reached out and picked up the maroon gotto. "If I can have just a minute, I'd like to put this thing on."

"But you too weak, Captain Jim," said Tahaleh. Her and Akbar were both pronouncing his name correctly. Zahra must have coached them, he thought.

Campbell thought about correcting her but let it go. He smiled up at her and said, "I'll lay back down when I've got this thing on. I feel a little vulnerable with no clothes. I'm sure it's psychological but, just the same, I'll feel better when I'm dressed."

"You will need help," said Zahra.

He looked up at her quickly. "Not from you, I don't!"

She smiled. "Come, Tahaleh. Let's leave the men for a few minutes." Tahaleh followed her out of the tent.

Campbell wrapped himself in the robe with no small amount of exertion. He sat breathlessly on the edge of the cot, winked at Akbar and, with his best confidential look, said, "Now what?"

Akbar looked at him quizzically. "What you mean?"

"I know you must have some kind of plan, right? I mean, how are you going to get the information to the good guys?"

Akbar cast his glance downward. "I am sorry, Captain Jim. I have no plan. This man was only contact in Kuwait. And I give to heem everything. He give to Americans and Saudis what I tell him."

"He must have had other people working with him?"

"Yes but who I don't know. Several women I think."

"I thought most of the women around here kept their faces hidden, their mouths shut, and performed only in the bedroom, and then only on command."

"That ees very true in many cases. I think that make it easier for women to hide secrets. Soldiers no suspect. This war change many things. I hear of many bad things in Kuwait. I think all Arab women say more when this war is gone."

"Let's find one who's talking now and get our information to the Allied Forces."

Akbar shook his head. "I do not know who can trust. It is too impossible."

"Then that means I've got to get through right away. Is

there any way you can help me?"

Akbar studied him for a long moment. "I weel take you to Kuwait's south border. I theenk maybe I know how to hide from soldiers. Many times I go Kuwait before war. My cousin live there."

Campbell felt the adrenaline build in his body. "When can we go?"

"As soon you strong to travel." Akbar leaned close. "You must give me time I tell Tahaleh. I think I tell her thees one tonight."

Campbell winked. "It's done, my friend." He held out his hand and Akbar shook it firmly, his excitement strong in his grip.

"You sleep now. We tell our friends our brother here. Very sick. You be sick."

Campbell smiled and lay back on the cot. "I'll be ready by tomorrow." He fell into a deep sleep almost as soon as his head touched the cot.

Campbell awakened to Zahra shaking him roughly. He opened his eyes and said, "Hey, take it easy. I'm awake. I'm awake."

The inside of the tent was almost dark. Campbell wasn't sure at first if it was early evening or morning. "What do you think you are doing?" said Zahra.

"I *was* sleeping."

"Tahaleh is crying her head off because Akbar has told her he is going to guide you to the southern border of Kuwait. He is all she has in this life. Let them live their lives out in peace. If he is discovered in Kuwait without papers, he'll be killed."

"He volunteered. I didn't twist his arm. I thought you said you were part of a resistance. Was that just lip service and chin music or are you really part of the resistance?"

Zhara hesitated. "There may be other ways to get your information to the Americans. Ways that Akbar doesn't know."

"And you do?"

"Maybe. I'm not sure yet."

"That's a little ambiguous. Why would you have a contact that Akbar doesn't know about?"

She glanced at the door. "I can't tell you that right now. I'm sorry."

"Okay, if you don't trust me, I can handle that, but what about Akbar? You don't trust him either?"

She shook her head. "No. It's not that I don't trust him. He's never met my contact."

"Where is he?"

"Baghdad."

"Baghdad? Are you crazy? I'm not going to Baghdad. I'm not into this spy business. I'll be in Saudi Arabia before you get back to Baghdad."

"Or you'll be dead – and Akbar with you – if he goes."

"Okay, he doesn't have to go. Maybe he can just draw me a map. I prefer that anyway. Are you satisfied?"

"Partially. I think you should stay with us until we can find a safe way to get you out of the country."

"No thanks. I'm not into Baghdad, or even one mile north of where we are right now. I prefer the desert."

"And the soldiers? And the tanks? And the mines? And the barbed wire? You will never make it. There are too many soldiers between here and Saudi Arabia."

Campbell experienced an odd feeling. He didn't know what it was, but he thought, for a moment, he had seen this woman a time he couldn't recall. He closed his eyes and searched for a picture. An image of blurred greys flashed before the eyes of his brain.

"Are you all right?"

He opened them. "Yeah, I'm fine. Where's Akbar? Let me talk to him."

"He and Tahaleh are near our fire. I'll ask them to come

in."

Campbell shook his head. "Just Akbar. Please."

She nodded and left the tent.

In a few moments all three of them entered the tent and stood by the cot. Campbell sat upright.

"Captain Jim," said Akbar. "Tahaleh and I, we talk of our plan. Tahaleh understands I must go."

Campbell looked from Akbar to Tahaleh. She smiled a tearful smile. "He must do this thing, Captain Jim."

Zahra's gaze met his, pleadingly.

Campbell cleared his throat. "Well, I've been thinking about this whole thing, Akbar. I think I might have a better chance if I went it alone. If you could draw me a map, I'd be all right."

"No, Captain Jim. That no work. In my plan we see a Kuwaiti woman. I think maybe she is resistance."

"Perhaps you can direct Captain Jim to her," said Zahra.

Akbar shook his head. "No. I go weeth him. We weel be safe. He weel be my deaf brother. We weel be safe. I weel leave heem in woman's hands. She get heem to Saudi Arabia. I come back safe."

The way Akbar said it left no room for dissension. Campbell studied their faces. He lingered on Zahra. *Something is missing here. I've had some kind of experience with you I can't remember.* "It's your decision, Akbar."

He smiled. "Good. When you are ready, we leave."

"I'll be ready in twenty-four hours, maybe less."

CHAPTER 10

Major Robert Wyman glanced at his instruments and let his mind wander in the darkness that surrounded him. He thought fondly of Buzz and the short time they had spent together while breaking Jim's code. His thoughts drifted to Jim. *If you're still alive, old friend, we'll get together when this is all over and we'll have the biggest celebration since the end of World War Two.*

His flight of F-18s from the *Coral Sea* patrolled Iraq's eastern boundary. In air-to-air configuration, they searched for Iraqi aircraft that might be attempting an escape into Iran. This was Wyman's big chance. With the F-18 configured for air-to-air combat, it was a match for anything Iraq had in the air. The only trouble was, there were no Iraqi aircraft in the sky.

Lieutenant Ed Townsend, normally Campbell's wingman, flew slightly behind Wyman's lead plane. Wyman had chewed him out pretty good for dropping down on the deck with Campbell when the latter had gone after the Iraqi Mig. Of course, Wyman would have done the same thing, had he been in a position to do so, but, as the flight leader, he couldn't admit that to his subordinate. He knew Ed felt guilty about losing Campbell, even though there was nothing he could have done against a missile.

Rudolph Redd's voice erupted in his headset. "Hey, Bob. We've got something on the screen at three-ten. Range about sixty miles. Heading is ninety-five. I've got no friendlies reported in that area."

Wyman keyed up for the rest of the squadron. "Dusty, this is Dusty One. Bogey at three-ten. Heading ninety-five. Range six-zero and closing left to right at five-thirty. Dusty Two and Three, stand by for confirmation of enemy target. Acknowlege.

Over."

"Dusty Two, roger."

"Dusty Three, ditto."

Wyman felt the excitement in their voices. He called Redd. "What's the word, Jeff?"

"MIG-29. She's flyin' flat out."

Wyman called his squadron. "Dusty One. Confirmed MIG-29 flat out." He paused. "This is going to be a little different than in the old days. I've never knocked a MIG out at sixty miles before. Dusty Two and Three, follow my lead. If I miss, Two gets next crack. Over."

"Dusty Two, roger."

"Dusty Three, gotcha,"

Wyman smiled. Thomas "Mutt" Posner and Rudolph "Jeff" Redd, two of the best pilots in the world, and they were willing to sit back calmly while he got the first shot. Of course he knew they hoped in some small way that he might miss so they could have their day but it was all in the spirit of becoming an ace. They wanted a kill but he knew they wanted him to get that fifth plane. Ed Townsend, the junior member of the team, remained silent. He would be fourth in line for a shot at the Mig.

Wyman acquired and locked onto the target. He fired a sidewinder missile and felt a slight change in pitch as the trim on the F-18 changed fractionally. He watched his radar digital display as the missile searched out its destination. The two blips converged on the screen and disappeared.

"Bingo! You got him, Skipper! He's gone as hell! Congratulations." It was a mixture of all three men speaking almost at the same time.

"Thanks." He paused briefly. "Dusty Leader to Dusty. Target destroyed. Resume routine."

The airwaves filled with salutations from the others in the air around him. Wyman felt a moment of elation as he realized he had reached the plateau of "ace", but the feeling didn't last. This wasn't like it had been in Vietnam. This time, he didn't even make visual contact with his enemy. There was no burst of adrenaline and flash of excitement as you fought it out, man-to-man, in the air. This was nothing more than a cold-blooded video game of death. How did he know for certain there had been an enemy aircraft? How did he know it wasn't a big joke?

The radio erupted. "Bogeys at thirty-five degrees. Range: 110. Direction: eighty-five. Speed: four hundred."

"How many?"

"Three. Two of 'em are big. Transports or bombers."

"Can we intercept before they make Iran?"

"Negative. They just crossed into Iranian airspace."

"Permission to attack targets?" It was Posner.

Wyman thought it over. If they fired their missiles at the fleeing enemy while the Marines were still in Iraqi airspace it would make no difference – the planes would still fall in Iran. Wyman wanted his men to have a shot, especially in light of his own victory, but he couldn't risk escalating the war.

"Negative, Mutt. Permission denied. We'll have another day."

He heard the disappointment in Posner's voice. "Roger."

Wyman checked his instruments. He keyed up. "Dusty, this is Dusty Leader. Re-form. Let's take it home."

They were five minutes into the return flight when radio silence was broken. "Jigsaw reports ground movement between here and the water – a column of vehicles – unknown types. The Kuwaiti Free Air Force spotted them but didn't have the fuel to engage. They want us to make a pass on our way back. The target is almost in line with our course."

"Do we have the fuel?"

"Roger."

"We can't do much more than a strafing run with the guns in this configuration, but we'll give it a go. Send the coordinates to the squadron."

Desert Fire

"Roger."

Wyman listened, almost absentmindedly, to the radio transmission as he searched out his lack of enthusiasm for the big number five – the one that made him an ace. He had waited almost twenty years for it and, now, he felt nothing. It was as though he had accomplished nothing more than washing the car or doing his laundry. *What the hell is life all about anyway? Why does someone look forward to killing someone else? I guess that's what I get for waiting twenty years to kill another man. I not only didn't get to see him, I didn't even see his plane.*

He made a small correction in his course to comply with the target coordinates. *It's just like a drill. It's clean and precise. We don't see them and, half the time, they probably don't see us.* They were over the target area. Wyman grimaced. *Yeah, mankind has sure come a long way in the art of making war.* He nosed the F-18 down and followed the blips on his night screen.

"Abort! Abort!" It was his own voice. He pulled back on the stick and felt the G-forces pull the blood from his head.

"Roger abort. What is it, Dusty Leader?" said Posner.

Wyman's voice wavered. "I can't confirm target as enemy."

Townsend, in Dusty Four, cut in. "There are no friendlies in the area, Skipper."

"I said I can't confirm the target! They may be civilians. The vehicles aren't large enough to be tanks or missile launchers."

"Civilians at this time of night?" said Townsend.

"There could be Allied prisoners in civilian vehicles down there." Wyman's voice was harsh. "Re-form the flight. Let's go home." All radios fell silent. They knew he was thinking of Campbell. They were all thinking of him.

The officer's mess was strained jubilant silence as the men in Wyman's flight took their morning coffee. Captain Redd was the first to make direct reference to the ground targets of only a few hours prior.

Stoney Livingston

"I think you were right, Pappy. Those targets were more like pickup trucks and cars than personnel carriers. Probably some of the resistance on maneuvers."

Wyman stared at his half-empty cup of coffee. "Yeah."

"I feel better about not hittin' 'em anyway," said Posner.

Wyman looked up at him. "Thanks, Mutt." He looked over at Redd. "You too, Jeff."

Townsend said thoughtfully. "You know, he's out there somewhere. We all know it. The Iraqis reported one POW killed in our attack on their 'milk factory'. Our sources said they had two Americans there. He got out. I know he did."

"No doubt about it, Pappy. If there was only one survivor in the whole damn factory, it would have to be Jim," said Redd.

An enlisted marine strode into the mess, impeccably tailored dress-blues announcing his advance. He stopped next to Wyman. "A message for Major Wyman, sir."

"What is it, Corporal?"

"You have a visitor topside, sir. On the flight deck."

"A visitor? Who is it?"

The corporal screwed up his face. "He said to tell you it was *First* Lieutenant Buzz, sir."

Instantly Wyman was on his feet, a smile on his face, his depression forgotten. "Lead the way, Corporal. I'm right behind you." He turned to the table. "If you gentlemen will excuse me." He turned and followed the immaculately dressed corporal, who was already halfway across the mess hall.

Buzz stood next to Wyman's F-18, proudly pointing to the freshly painted Iraqi flag below the canopy, next to four North Vietnamese flags. "Congratulations." He extended his hand warmly.

Wyman shook his hand firmly and pointed to the silver bars on Buzz's collars. "Congratulations yourself. Welcome to the Corps."

The corporal turned and marched stiffly away.

Desert Fire

Buzz pointed to 'number five' and said, "They were still painting it on when I got here. I can actually tell my grandkids I saw number five go on one of the last airplanes to ever be flown by an ace. There won't be very many in this war I don't think."

"Forget that. What in the hell are you doing here? And how long can you stay?"

"I've gotta go back to the salt mines tomorrow but I wanted to tell you a bit of good news. And, since I know a man of great influence, I was able to arrange a chopper ride out here." Buzz winked.

Wyman felt his heart quicken. He punched Buzz on the shoulder. "What is it? You got news of Jim?"

Buzz nodded. "We think he's alive and has escaped."

Wyman felt his eyes light up.

Buzz held up his hands. "He hasn't shown up inside our lines yet but we intercepted an Iraqi radio transmission a couple of days ago that indicated someone had engaged an Iraqi PC in a firefight. The transmission from the PC went dead right after the initial message."

"What makes you think it was Jim?" Wyman felt disappointment.

"The initial transmission from the Iraqi PC indicated they had discovered one of their PCs abandoned by the side of the road. They had a firefight with one of their own PCs!"

Wyman felt his hopes rising again.

"It took me a while to put it together but we caught a radio transmission on low frequency just after daylight the night we hit the 'milk factory'. The Iraqis were looking for a missing PC. They couldn't account for it in the damage assessment."

Wyman's emotions hit the heights. "It's Jim! I know it is. What happened after the firefight?"

"We don't know but, if they captured or killed him, it would have been front page. They don't have a whole lot to brag about so far in this war."

Wyman grinned and said, "You feel like a drink?"

"You got one?"

"I might."

"Let's do it."

They sat on deck, both staring into the waters of the Persian Gulf. Several moments of silence followed a toast to Campbell. Buzz spoke first. "What are you going to do when this one's over?"

Wyman took a sip of his bourbon and coke from a coffee cup. He stared wistfully at the horizon. "Hell, I don't know, Buzz. I guess I'll quit the Corps at the end of this one."

"And do what? Retire?"

"I've got enough time in. I don't have many expenses. I've got a house damn near paid for outside of Sacramento. Who knows? I might look for a little color in the hills around there. With gold as high as it is now, a guy could scratch out a decent living if he knew what he was doing."

"You know, Bob, you could be the last man to ever become an ace. Have you ever thought of that?"

Wyman took another sip from his cup. "Yeah, I have. And it doesn't mean a damned thing to me anymore." He turned to face Buzz. "Do you know I never even saw the other plane? Oh yeah, I saw it on radar, but I didn't really *see* it. If we can do that to them, then they can do it to us. I could be flying along some night – fat, dumb and happy – and boom! No more ace fighter pilot. Naw, when this one's over, I'm a civilian. I'll find something to do."

"You ever think about intelligence?"

"I told you I was getting out."

"I mean as a civilian."

Wyman shook his head. "Not me. I don't want anything to do with codes or spies or any of that other stuff. I wanna kick back and take it easy. Might teach private pilots – start my own little business. I don't know for sure but, whatever I do, it won't have anything to do with the government – ours or anybody else's."

Buzz sipped his bourbon and water. "What about Campbell? What do you think he'll do if he gets back?"

"He'll get back."

"I mean *when* he gets back."

"I don't know. We talked a time or two about starting up a little flight school. Only trouble is Jim doesn't have near enough time to retire and, even worse, he wants to set the business up in New Mexico. Me, I want to see the snow on the peaks of the mountains year 'round."

"So you think he might want to get out too, huh? "

"You can never be sure about things like that but Jim was never very military with his bearing. To tell you the truth, I don't know how he ever made captain. Oh, he's got the smarts, sure, but he's been chewed out by some of the biggest brass in the Corps. He's broken about every rule he could find, then looked for more. He knows his days in the Corps are numbered. You ought to see him fly that F-18." Wyman felt the pride in his voice as he talked about his friend.

"I always say how I'm the greatest and all of that garbage but I do it as a joke. Hell, there must be at least one or two in the Corps almost as good as I am. Jim is one of them.

"Jim is the best I ever saw. I don't know how he gets the airplane to do some of the things he gets it to do. The way I figure it, he should have busted about three or four of 'em right in half. But he keeps doing it, and the plane keeps letting him get away with it." Wyman grinned as he thought of Campbell. "I don't think I could afford to start up a flight school with him now that I think about it. He'd rip the wings off of everything we could buy commercially."

"My cup's empty."

Wyman leaned over and picked up the bottle of bourbon. He poured the cup half full.

Stoney Livingston

Buzz looked at him quizzically. "What? No water?"

"Too far to walk."

Buzz grunted. "You're right." He sipped gingerly as he stared at the water off the bow. "What about girlfriends or marriage?"

"Goddamn, Buzz, are you some kind of cub reporter for a big newspaper? Give the intelligence section a break. Loosen up."

"I was just curious, that's all."

"Well, it's no big deal I guess. I've got at least twenty girlfriends in fifteen countries, including the States. Some of 'em matured with me so to speak. But nothing serious." He clucked. "I'm gonna miss a lot of 'em but that's the way it goes I guess." He poured himself some more bourbon.

"How about you, Buzz? What the hell you gonna do?"

"I think I'll stay in for a while. Who knows? I might even earn my own name one of these days. My father will be retiring shortly and it looks like I'll carry on the family tradition."

Wyman felt the effects of the liquor. "War sucks, Buzz."

"I think Sherman said 'War is hell'."

"I don't give a damn what Sherman said. *I* said war sucks."

"Succinctly put, sir. More contemporary than what Sherman said anyway."

Wyman clamped his jaws together. "Here we sit, talking trash, drinking American bourbon, and contemplating the future, and Jim is out there somewhere, probably dying of thirst."

"So what the hell would he have us do? Sit around and mope all day?"

Wyman smiled. "Good point. Damn good point. You know what ol' Jim would say to that? 'Let's get ripped and forget about what we can't do anything about.' He's that way about shit. You know what I mean?"

"Maybe you ought to take a lesson from him on that one."

"You ever been on a carrier before, Buzz?"

140

Desert Fire

"Nope."

"What d'ya think?"

"About what?"

"About anything, damnit."

"When do you fly next?"

"That's what you think?"

"No, but I'm a little worried that maybe we should quit drinking now."

Wyman poured them both another drink. "Don't sweat it, Buzz, old man. I'm a hero for a day or two. They gave me a whole twenty-four hours off. Like I really did something up there."

"You got number five."

"I'd trade it for Jim Campbell in a heartbeat." As soon as the words left his mouth, Wyman realized what was bothering him. All his military life he had dreamed of being an ace fighter pilot. When the day finally came, it was no longer important – not even a little bit important. Twenty years of waiting culminated in disappointment. A friend meant more to him than his life's dream.

He faced Buzz, who sat silently. "That's it, Buzz. That's the bottom line. Nothing means a damn thing without your buddies. It doesn't matter if your buddy is a wife or a girlfriend or a guy in the same outfit, or all three. What the hell does anything matter without your real friends?"

Buzz lifted his coffee cup. "To real friends."

Wyman touched his cup to Buzz's and downed what he had left. "After this war is over, let's all of us get together. What do you say? We'll get a bunch of girls and have a helluva party – laugh about this whole thing."

"Sounds like a plan to me," said Buzz, his words a bit longer than normal.

"What say we invite Mutt and Jeff?"

"The guys you told me about?"

"None other." Wyman looked out to sea then turned back to Buzz. "How would you like to meet a couple of the best pilots in

141

the world?"

    Buzz emptied his cup. "Shit. Let's do it."

CHAPTER 11

Campbell watched Akbar's body sway back and forth with the movement of the camel. He urged his own mount a little closer. "The guys in my outfit will never believe this. I'm the one doing it and I'm not so sure *I* believe it. I thought the only real camels were cigarettes."

Akbar turned slightly on his perch and smiled. "You are a man with good humor, Captain Jim. It does you well. Maybe when we are finish this war, we be good friends."

"Ow! Hell, we could be damn good friends right now if you'd tell this cantankerous animal to quit trying to bite me. I think I was better off on foot."

"Camel carry more food and water than man. Soldiers no look for American pilot on camel."

"Point well taken, Akbar. And one that's keepin' this miserable excuse for a horse alive." He paused. "You don't suppose we could trade this one in on a later model, do you?"

"My cousin not happy if we do that. You have him best camel."

"The man has my sympathies."

The mood was jovial, almost carefree, as they rode the camels along the highway. Campbell felt physically better than he had since before his capture.

They entered Kuwait in the darkness, moving toward the main road that led to Kuwait City. Akbar said he kind of knew the way but wasn't really certain. He led more by instinct than any concrete knowledge, avoiding areas he thought might be good places for mine fields. Campbell was content to allow Akbar the

143

lead as he had no knowledge of his own that would be any better than Akbar's instinct. They stopped in the middle of the night, against Campbell's wishes, but Akbar assured him that anyone moving about at this late hour would be highly suspect if stopped by any of Hussein's army. They made camp in the sand, not far from a large road, even lighting a fire to heat their food. Akbar said it would be less suspicious if they acted as expected.

They had just finished eating when a solitary soldier entered their camp. The man was afoot and appeared bedraggled and exhausted. He pointed his rifle at Campbell and spoke rapidly. When no response was forthcoming, he jabbed Campbell in the ribs with his rifle barrel. Akbar spoke to the soldier rapidly and with the proper amount of indignation, explaining, Campbell was certain, that his brother was a deaf mute and not in the best of health. The soldier eyed them both suspiciously for a moment, then ignored Campbell and spoke at length with Akbar.

Campbell watched the soldier for any sign the man might tire of the conversation and begin shooting his rifle. He thought of his own AK-47, lying inconspicuously hidden beneath his bedroll. It was too far out of reach if this guy started shooting. He fingered the knife at his waist, under the robe. It would be awkward but, if he worked his hand under the robe inconspicuously, he might be able to hurt this guy. He wondered why this soldier was alone and where his unit was located.

Suddenly the soldier raised his voice. Campbell didn't have to speak the language to know something was not going well. Akbar replied in a loud, defensive tone to whatever the soldier had said. The soldier swung his rifle butt, striking Akbar in the ribs, knocking him to the sand,

Campbell covered the two or three yards between them and plunged his knife into the man's ribs, striking bone as the blade penetrated the heart. He wiggled the knife up and down, side-to-side, withdrew it and slit the exposed throat.

Akbar picked himself from the ground and knelt next to the

dead soldier. He looked up at Campbell. "He ees very dead."

Campbell wiped the blade of his knife on the inside of his robe. "I didn't like the way things were going."

"You were right. He was going to keel us and take our camels. I theenk he was a deserter. Maybe too many bombs from your air force."

Campbell thought about what Akbar had said for a moment. "That could mean a lot of things. We may be whippin' the hell out of 'em and they're about to give it up, or this guy was a wimp and left his buddies to save his own life. Either way, we can't expect much in the way of consideration if we have a bunch of panic-stricken soldiers headed our way. They'll kill and take what they want."

"What you say is true, Captain Jim. I Theenk we are in greater danger than I thought."

Campbell smiled. "That's not the best English in the world but you got your point across."

"We must hide his body in the sand."

They dug a shallow grave in silence. Campbell felt an odd remorse when they placed the body in the narrow hole in the ground. He wondered if the soldier had been a kind man under normal circumstances. War and fear and panic often caused great changes in men. He would never know for certain but he liked to think this particular soldier was not a kind man. It made him feel better about what he had done.

At first light they continued their journey. They moved through and among the soldiers of Hussein's army without drawing any special attention. There were refugees all around them; most were Kuwaitis, made homeless by Iraq's invasion, but some were nomads like Akbar.

The civilians were all on the move but Campbell couldn't figure out where they were going, and whether they were going from or to someplace. Many drove cars, others motorcycles or bicycles; some rode camels or horses pulling carts with all their worldly possessions. Then there were those who walked aimlessly about, seemingly unsure of where they were going or what they were doing; not really caring.

A military roadblock on the road ahead caused Campbell's heartbeat rate to increase. Akbar spoke to him softly. "Do not worry. Be silent. I weel talk for both of us."

Campbell pulled his hood further over his head and rode by Akbar's side, his heart pounding in his temples. Ahead lay Kuwait City. There Campbell was supposed to get papers that would allow him to travel more freely as a Kuwaiti Citizen. The roadblock was his last obstacle.

Three soldiers motioned them to stop. Akbar held his animal back but made no attempt to dismount. One of the three soldiers moved to Akbar's camel and went through his bags, another to Campbell's mount. All the while, Akbar and the third soldier carried on a steady stream of conversation.

Campbell glanced at the soldier searching his bags but made no attempt to prolong eye contact. The AK-47 strapped to the inside of his robe chafed at him, the sharp edges of the magazine poking him in the ribs. He straightened his body so the robe hung more loosely, defining no bulges or strange protrusions through the thick material.

The soldier looked up at him and smiled. He held up a bag of dates and said something. Campbell looked at him dumbly and smiled, as he had practiced per Zahra's instructions. The soldier seemed irritated. He repeated whatever it was he had said before, his voice louder and more demanding. Campbell continued to smile at him dumbly.

Akbar's voice broke in. The soldier looked at him, then back to Campbell. He smiled and pointed to the bag of dates, then pointed to his mouth. Campbell smiled and nodded. The soldier took the dates and walked away, searching the road for his next approaching victim. In another moment, the two were bid farewell, Akbar's fee being a small portion of dried goat meat.

Desert Fire

Out of earshot of the soldiers, Campbell said, "This must be prime duty. I think those guys were more interested in food than anything else." He thought of the Allied mission. "We must be hurtin' 'em from the air."

"It is not good in Kuwait City. The soldier told me we don't want go there." Akbar screwed up his face as he searched for the proper English word. "Many Brutallies."

"Brutalities."

"Yes, that too."

Campbell smiled, his brush with the enemy already a part of his mind's history.

"Soldier say much killing, stealing. They take woman when they want. Big party to some soldiers."

Campbell gritted his teeth. "Yeah, well, I hope they have a good time, 'cause when it comes time to pay the bill, I think they're gonna be a little short on cash."

"What that mean, Captain Jim?"

"Means they're gonna be real sorry when this is all over and we've whipped their butts back to Baghdad."

Akbar smiled. "I theenk so too."

They rode in silence, the outline of the city growing on the horizon. "After a while, Campbell said, "Hey, Akbar, how come you and Tahaleh and Zahra are involved in this resistance thing? I mean, I know about Zahra's boyfriend and your family, but a person has to have a hope of winning to get involved in something like a revolution – at least I would think they would. What if we pull up without taking Hussein out of power? What will you do then?"

A sad look came over his face. "We fight on. It ees better we die a free man than leeve with fear like baby in night. We want nothing but freedom. No care about politics. No care about Jews. Care about food and water. Shelter. Place to teach children."

"School?"

"That too."

Campbell smiled. "I imagine that Zahra would be one helluva teacher."

Akbar nodded. "Zahra number one teacher – English, mathematics, geography." He cast a side-glance at Campbell. "Pretty too, huh?"

"Pretty too, yes. No doubt about that."

"I theenk you like Zahra."

"Of course I like Zahra. I like you and Tahaleh too."

"Not same kind of like. I hope for you sake. Akbar is man. Tahaleh my wife."

Campbell laughed. "I didn't mean I liked her that way."

"Who? Tahaleh or Zahra?"

"Neither."

Akbar shook his head. "Then you not so smart I theenk you are. Zahra smartest, prettiest woman in Iraq, except for Tahaleh."

Campbell rode in silence for several minutes. "What happened the night Tahaleh found me?"

"Zahra no tell?"

Campbell shook his head.

"You ask her. She weel tell."

"Hell, Akbar, you know I'll never see her again. What's the big deal?"

"No beeg deal. Maybe you write her letter. She write good."

"Damnit, Akbar, why do I get the impression you're avoiding the issue here?"

"Maybe because eet is so."

"Oh." Again they rode on in silence.

Akbar pointed to the south. "I theenk we go thees way and come to ceety from south. Stay away from airport. Too many soldiers there."

"What about mines?"

"Mines okay eef we go now." Akbar nudged his camel off

148

the road and into the sand.

Campbell wondered what difference it made when they went. If there were mines, they would be mindless of the time of day they exploded. He said nothing, but strained his eyes, searching for any signs of disturbance in the sand before him as the heavily laden animals plowed through the desert. The trip around the airport added three hours to their approach to the city but they arrived safely on the outskirts of the southern city limits shortly before dark.

Campbell had the sensation he was in a fantasy world as the two rode into town on a mode of transportation almost as ancient as the arrival of man in this region of the world. The modern streets and buildings stood in stark contrast to their dress and the animals beneath them.

Akbar leaned close and spoke softly. "I have cousin here. We turn next street."

Campbell nodded and fell in behind Akbar. Further conversation was dangerous. Some of the buildings facing the street had fresh bullet holes in the walls. Several were missing panes of glass. One had a huge hole in the wall. Campbell looked through the hole and into the interior of the house where it appeared the family was eating and carrying on with life as though the wall was still in place.

The soft thuds of the camels' feet on the paved road were the only sounds as the two turned to the right and proceeded down the street between a neat row of houses. Campbell was surprised at the affluence displayed in the construction and landscaping of the homes. He wanted to ask Akbar a hundred questions but held his tongue in check. It would wait.

They stopped the camels four houses from a corner and dismounted, Campbell waiting for Akbar to perform the feat first and give the command for his own animal to kneel. It felt good to stand on the ground, even though it seemed to sway for a moment before settling down. Campbell touched the rifle through his robe and felt comforted.

A plump woman appeared at the door of the house next to which they stood, her face covered by a veil. Campbell saw her eyes smile as she recognized Akbar. She rushed to greet him as Campbell stood silently nearby, looking at the surrounding houses absentmindedly. He heard Akbar's voice and turned back to them. The woman looked at him, her eyes showing suspicion above the veil.

Akbar said softly in English. "We go into house now. Follow."

Campbell nodded and fell in behind them as they walked through the door. The inside of the house was a bigger surprise to him than the outward appearance had been. He wasn't sure what he had been expecting but it wasn't what he found.

The house was ornately furnished in the finest wood: mahogany from the Philippines, teak from Indonesia, burl from the forests of China. A thick Persian carpet covered the floor in the main room of the house. Campbell would call it a living room but he wasn't sure what they called it. Pictures and paintings framed in dark woods adorned the cloth-wallpapered walls. A Louis the Fourteenth chair occupied a place of importance near a teak secretary desk.

The woman motioned to an early eighteenth century sofa. Campbell followed Akbar's lead and sat gingerly in the firm period piece. Akbar spoke rapidly to the woman. Campbell heard his name. The woman seemed momentarily in awe of him.

Akbar faced him. "Captain Jim, I give to you my cousin, Fatemeh Amin. Fatemeh, Captain Jim."

Fatemeh extended her plump hand. Campbell stood and shook it warmly. She pulled away quickly and disappeared into another room.

He looked down at Akbar, still sitting on the sofa. "Where'd she go?"

"She goes get food. Make children hide camels."

"How the hell do you hide a camel?"

"Have good place. Not far. You call like barn in your country."

"Oh. Where's her husband?"

"He is at meeting. Back soon. We wait. Eat."

Campbell took in more of his surroundings. "They don't do too bad for themselves, do they?"

"What that mean?"

"I mean, they aren't poor."

Akbar smiled. "No. Ali work for oil company. Chemical engineer. Big smart." He curled his lip in a smile. "No can ride camel so good."

Campbell returned the smile. "Doesn't look to me like this guy has to ride a camel."

"He ride American car. Cadillac."

"I'll be damned." He shook his head. "Only in the Middle East – a camel and a Cadillac parked in the same garage."

"What you mean?"

"Never mind."

Fatemeh rushed into the room, babbling rapidly. Campbell jumped to his feet and searched Akbar's face for a reaction. He didn't have long to wait.

"Soldiers! They are come to this house now. We hide."

Campbell lifted the robe and unhooked the AK-47. Fatemeh's face showed her fear.

Akbar spoke to her soothingly. He turned to Campbell. "Come. We have place hide. In other room."

Campbell followed him to an adjoining room where Fatemeh swung a large bookcase outward, revealing a passageway into the wall. The two men stepped into the darkened space and Fatemeh quickly swung the bookcase back into position.

In the darkness of the confined space, Campbell smelled his own body odor and that of Akbar's, mixed with the smell of camel and the light coat of oil on his AK-47. He held his breath, listening for sounds from within the house. He was thankful the children were away with the camels. The fewer people to be confronted by the soldiers, the less their chances of discovery.

Feint sounds of people talking rapidly grew louder as the voices moved into the room with the large bookcase. Campbell fought his fear at the thought of being discovered like a trapped rat. He couldn't be sure but it sounded to him like there were two male voices and that of Fatemeh's. One of the soldier's voices grew harsh. Fatemeh answered him angrily. The second soldier said something. Fatemeh fell silent. He felt Akbar stiffen at his side. He checked his urge to ask Akbar what was going on.

The angry soldier said something. Fatemeh answered. There was a pleading tone in her voice, unmistakable, even to Campbell. The sounds of a struggle, followed by the ripping of cloth and the muffled screams of Fatemeh, mixed with the laughter of the soldiers enraged Campbell. He felt Akbar at his side, trembling. Campbell closed his eyes. A picture of Zahra flashed before him. She was naked. A soldier was on top of her. He picked up the soldier's rifle and put it to the man's temple. The picture went black.

Campbell opened his eyes in the darkness of their hiding place and reached under his robe. He pulled out the knife that had served him so well on other occasions. Fatemeh's muffled cries bored into his brain. Akbar held his arm. Campbell jerked it free and pushed the bookcase open.

Fatemeh was on her back on the floor. One of the soldiers knelt at her head, one hand covering her mouth, the other fondling her exposed breasts. The other lay between her spread legs, his trousers down around his knees as he tried to force his way inside her squirming body.

Campbell slit the throat of the man at Fatemeh's head as quickly and effortlessly as slicing a pat of butter. Blood poured onto Fatemeh and the Persian carpet from the severed jugular as

Desert Fire

Campbell jumped at the other soldier. The man rolled off his intended victim but, with his trousers wrapped around his knees, his fate was sealed. He Barely had time to loose one short and desperate cry from his lips before Campbell's knife did its work. The scream bubbled to silence as the soldier choked and drowned in his own blood, a look of fear and surprise on his dying face. The body collapsed to the floor and jerked spasmodically in a last fight against death but it lost the battle and lay still after a few seconds.

Fatemeh whimpered softly behind him. He turned and saw Akbar wrapping her in the remnants of her clothing, speaking to her softly. She looked up at Campbell and spoke softly in her native tongue and left the room quietly. He didn't ask Akbar to interpret her words.

"Let's get them out of here," he said.

Akbar was already pushing the bodies to the side of the room, rolling up the bloody carpet. "We must work fast. They were looking for Ali. They suspect him of something."

"Where are her kids? And how many does she have?"

"They should be back quick. Two boys. They come soon."

Campbell grunted under the weight of one of the bodies as he moved it to the rear of the house, wrapped in the carpet, Akbar on the other end of the grizzly load. They dumped the body in a shed behind the house and repeated the procedure. Kneeling over the second body, Campbell looked at Akbar. "Now what?"

"We must get camels. Take bodies far away and bury in sand."

Campbell looked into Akbar's eyes. "I've caused you folks a lot of grief, haven't I?"

"This was not for you. They suspect Ali of resistance movement."

Campbell looked down at one of the bodies. A fly perched at the edge of the gash on the dead man's throat. Campbell brushed it away. "I know what happened that night Tahaleh found me. I remembered when we were hiding in that closet."

"It is not for talk about now."

Campbell clenched and unclenched his fist. He looked at Akbar. "This can be one shitty place to be a woman."

"Not talk about it now. We have work."

"Tell her I know."

"Yes, yes. I tell her. Now I go get camels."

The sun was almost below the horizon. Campbell looked south. "I'll help you load the bodies but I'm not going with you to bury them. I'm going to Saudi Arabia."

"But the papers and transport?"

"I figure the border is only about ninety or a hundred miles away. Two nights on foot if I'm lucky."

Akbar struggled to convert the miles into kilometers. "There are too many soldiers."

"I've got to get back. Time is of the essence. I've got a lot of information to get to the Coalition. I'm not waiting any longer, Akbar. I can't."

Fatemeh stepped through the back door of the house, dressed in fresh clothing. She spoke rapidly but quietly with Akbar for a moment. When she finished, she looked at Campbell. Akbar interpreted. "She want thank you very deeply from her heart. She know war bring out much bad in people. Tell you she know not all Iraqi bad like two soldiers. She say you good American, Captain Jim. When war is done, you and your family welcome her home."

Campbell felt his emotions wash to the surface. He was tired of the inhumanity all around him, and to hear this woman so quickly find good in most Iraqis was almost more than he could handle. He fought back the tears and nodded to her. "Tell her I will be proud to visit her family when this war is over and, if I ever have a family of my own, I will bring them with me. Tell her she is welcome in my home too."

Akbar translated his words to Fatemeh. She smiled weakly

and said something to Akbar who turned back to Campbell. "She say we go now. Allah be with us."

Campbell wiped his eyes with the back of his hand. "Go get the camels. I'll wait here."

The quiet of the night was broken by sporadic gunfire from the city. Akbar sat silently in the darkness, two fresh mounds of dirt next to where he sat. Campbell took a drink of water from a goatskin bag.

"Burying people is thirsty work, huh, Akbar?"

"You no have to act tough. I know this is bother you."

"Okay, so what the hell do we talk about now – the college basketball season? I think new Mexico State's got a pretty damn good team, but I think Seton Hall or UNLV is going to walk away with the NCAA. What do you think?"

"I no understand."

"I didn't think so. That's what I was trying to say. What do we have in common besides war and killing?"

"War, maybe. Killing, I don't know. You do it so fast, I no have time to kill anybody."

"That makes me feel better. Not the killin' – the fact you didn't have to do any of it."

"For this I am happy."

There was a long pause.

"You are certain you want try get back Saudi alone?"

"Yeah, I'm certain."

"You have anything last you want say?"

Campbell closed his eyes. Zahra was there, the Iraqi soldier over her. He popped open his eyes and looked at Akbar. "Maybe I do but I don't know how to say it."

Akbar nodded. "I understand. English difficult language."

Despite his thoughts, Campbell smiled. "That's not exactly what I meant."

"You tell me then."

"It's about Zahra."

"What about Zahra?"

Campbell hesitated, searching for the right words. "If I get a chance, I'd like to see her again. Do you think she would mind? I mean after the war is over and things are more settled."

He could see Akbar's exposed teeth as the Bedouin smiled broadly. "I think she like see you. Maybe not make good wife until older though. She have very strong mind. How you say? She have one hard head."

Campbell chuckled and stood. "My friend, I better be going. I owe you more than I can ever repay."

"Maybe someday you pay if you my brother. Marry Zahra, then you have to be my brother." He stood.

The two embraced. "So long, Brother," said Campbell.

"May Allah be with you, Captain Jim. I tell Zahra you talk of her."

Campbell picked up two goatskin water bags and a pouch of dried food and marched into the night without looking back at Akbar.

CHAPTER 12

Campbell moved swiftly in the night, aided by a dim partial moon, unafraid of mines, tired of the grown-up game of war. As the first grey light of day made its way to the sky on the eastern horizon, he stopped and dug in for the long day ahead, to wait for another night to come. He was grateful for the respite but anxious to get back to freedom on the other side of the Kuwaiti border. He had seen no troops in the course of his march that first night after he had parted company with Akbar.

During the day, his thoughts ran the gamut from childhood experiences to his recent farewell to Akbar. The man hardly knew him and yet he was willing to risk everything, including his life, to aid in his escape. *We're fighting the Iraqis. Akbar's an Iraqi. War sure as hell makes for strange alliances.*

Zahra passed through his mind more than once during the course of the day, but he quickly forced his mental wanderings in other directions. He didn't want to dwell on her just yet. He knew the time would come when he would force total recall, but now was not the time.

He thought of his maternal grandparents and imagined that he could communicate with them using telepathy. He concentrated his thoughts and sent them flying with an early-afternoon wind that kicked up sand and dust, much as his thoughts would if they reached his grandfather.

The wind picked up in the mid-afternoon and, by late afternoon, visibility was less than two hundred yards. The small bits of sand stung when they struck Campbell, even through the thickness of his robe. Despite his closed eyes, some of the dust particles made their way underneath his eyelids, causing extreme discomfort.

With visibility so poor, Campbell decided to take a chance and continue his journey before dark. The quicker he put the miles behind him, the quicker he'd be in Saudi Arabia.

The wind continued to grow stronger and by nightfall was a howling storm. Campbell leaned forward at an extreme angle to keep from being blown over backwards by the strong gusts as he trudged south. Nothing but the wind and sand seemed to occupy the land around him. *Where in the hell is the Iraqi army?*

The wind died down after midnight and visibility improved. During the storm Campbell had continued his trek using dead reckoning. When he was again able to see the stars, he found himself right on course. He wasn't certain of the distance he had covered but at least he had been going in the right direction.

He stopped for a drink of water and a small amount of dried meat. When he completed his meal, he headed east. He was almost positive he was in Saudi Arabia and if he walked east until he ran into the ocean he could then turn south and walk the short distance to Khafji, the northernmost town on the Saudi Arabian coast. There was a small detachment of marines there with the Saudi and Kuwaiti troops. Campbell felt warm inside as he thought of a reunion with friendly forces, especially marines.

As he trudged the bleakness of the desert at night, he wondered if he had been spotted by ground radar or sentries on either side. He found it odd that he had encountered no activity, even taking the storm into consideration. *Is the war over? Naw, couldn't be. Those Iraqi soldiers wouldn't have been in Kuwait. Not unless the politicians have gone south, like they did during the Vietnam war. It couldn't have happened that fast.*

What if we started the invasion and took heavy casualties? That might do it. The American people still don't understand that war means dying.

The smell of salt water reached him. Surely, someone would have sentries out on the main highway. The highway roughly paralleled the coastline from Bahrain, Saudi Arabia in the south to Kuwait City in the north, running through the center of Khafji near the northern Saudi border. Campbell stopped short of the highway and turned south. He moved more cautiously, afraid now of being shot by friendly forces. *That's the trouble with bullets -- they can't tell the good guys from the bad.*

A faint whirring sound reached him. It appeared to originate from behind him. *They've spotted me! Now if I can just convince them I'm on their side before they dust me off, I'll be okay.* The fear of uncertainty crept into his throat. He hid behind a small mound of dirt as the sound grew louder.

He formulated one plan after the other but none of them appealed to him – they were all too risky. The whirring sound of the engine soon became apparent as two engines, then three, then four, then too many to count by sound. *Jesus! Are they sending a whole mechanized division after one man? I mean, I knew it was boring out here, but this is ridiculous.*

The sounds of the moving vehicles grew in intensity until all other sounds, save an occasional creak of heavy tracked vehicles, were drowned out by the straining engines. Campbell crawled to the crest of the small mound and searched the landscape. A mechanized column of armored vehicles, tanks, personnel carriers and self-propelled guns stretched as far as he could see. He dropped back behind the mound. *Holy shit! Iraqis!* He tried to make sense out of it. *Maybe I got lost in the storm for a while and drifted off course. I must still be in Kuwait. Damn!*

He went over and over the time and distance in his mind, but could not reconcile what he saw with what he thought his position was. He peeked over the mound again. The bulk of the column moved south on the road, less than a half-mile from his position. A few tracked vehicles seemed randomly spread to the sides of the column. Campbell dropped back behind the mound. *Damnit, I know I'm in Saudi Arabia. What the hell are they doing down here? I can't believe they're invading. Are they crazy?*

Stoney Livingston

Where the hell are the guys on our team? Am I dreaming? What's going on?

He sat for several moments, unsure of what his next move should be. *I've got to keep them in sight. If I lose them, they could set up positions and I might walk into 'em.*

One of the flanking tracked personnel carriers moved within a hundred yards of his position. Campbell jumped to his feet and made a mad dash for the slow-moving vehicle. *A BMP armored personnel carrier. It could have been worse.* He could see the silhouette of a man's head and upper shoulders in the center of the turret housing the 73-mm rocket gun. The man seemed to be looking forward, intent on what lay ahead, unconcerned about his back.

The APC slowed as it climbed a steep dune. Campbell reached up and grabbed the pull ring located on the rear of the vehicle. He hung on for life as the unit picked up speed on the down side of the dune. His rifle barrel beat him mercilessly in the back of the head as it bounced around his back on a loose sling. At the bottom of the dune, the APC swerved right, nearly jerking Campbell's grip loose, but he managed to get his other hand into position to grab the ring, disregarding the rifle swinging on his back. With all the strength he could muster, he pulled himself onto the heavy metal deck of the personnel carrier. He checked the man in the turret. *Still there.*

Campbell could see only the top of the back of the soldier's head. The large round hatch on the BMP swings up and to the rear, cutting rearward visibility for anyone using the turret for observation. In Campbell's case, it worked well as a shield between him and the man in the turret.

Campbell moved forward to the small turret and sat directly behind and below the hatch. He smiled at his own brazenness. Below him, in the passenger compartment of the personnel carrier, he knew there was a squad, or maybe more. When the thought made its way to his consciousness, Campbell felt a tingling sensation in his testicles, like standing too close to the top edge of a tall building. It was a kind of fear that wasn't controllable, yet it was the kind of fear that wasn't immediate. *No sense worrying about getting hurt until after the fall starts.*

Fear of the driver suddenly turning the turret caused him to move back a few feet. It put him at greater risk of being discovered, but it lessened his chances of getting caught by a sudden movement of the turret. He consciously controlled his breathing until he recovered from his mad dash and climb onto the APC.

Campbell sat, almost nonchalantly, on the rear deck of the APC. He figured if he was spotted in the darkness, he would be taken as one of the crew by a casual observer. He was tempted to ask the man in the turret for a cigarette, but his confidence fell short of that move.

The column continued to move south at a high rate of speed. The flanking vehicles were unable to keep up with the pace and fell slowly behind. *What the hell kind of an advance is this? I can't believe we haven't taken these guys out yet. Where is everybody?*

Khafji lay only two or three miles directly in front of them. He *was* in Saudi Arabia. *What happened? Did we call it quits and go home? And these guys are moving in to occupy Saudi Arabia too?*

An explosion near the front of the column sent a flash of light into the night. They were less than a mile from Khafji. *It's about time!*

The column in front of him broke and scattered to the sides of the road but continued south. The APC beneath him continued on course, trying to catch up with the main element. More explosions racked the night. The Iraqi tanks in the lead opened up with their main guns. Suddenly the night was ablaze. Illumination canisters popped overhead and the night became day.

Stoney Livingston

Campbell's heart jumped into his throat as the man in the turret turned to look behind him and spotted his unauthorized cargo. Campbell fired a short burst and saw the soldier's face collapse into itself, a dark, runny liquid flowing down what only seconds before had been a face. The body crumpled out of sight into the APC. Campbell jumped from the fast-moving vehicle and did a shoulder roll upon impact with the ground. He was up and running to the west before his forward movement stopped.

The Iraqi APC did not pursue for unknown reasons. Perhaps they thought the observer had been killed by enemy fire from a much greater range than six or seven feet.

Only when his lungs and legs could no longer support his flight of fear, did Campbell stop running. He fell to the ground and gasped in huge gulps of air, the sounds of the battle obscured by his own heavy breathing. After several minutes, the pounding in his chest and throat subsided and he lay quietly in the sand, expecting at any moment to see a tank or an APC rolling over the desert at his supine form.

There was nothing but a slight breeze. That and his fear. He rolled to his stomach and checked the action on his AK-47. He pulled the magazine and ejected each round. *Only nineteen left.* Deliberately and with a new surge of energy, he reloaded the magazine and inserted it back into the rifle, then stood and moved toward the city of Khafji in a crouch, on the alert for troops from either side. He saw neither, only the Iraqi armored vehicles on or near the road east of him. Some of the Iraqis had gained the outer limits of the city. *Come on, guys! Where's the counter-attack?*

On the western edge of town, Campbell knelt near a gas station, surveying what he could of the battle. He determined rifle fire from inside the city but couldn't tell if it was coming from the invading Iraqis or the city's defenders. When he realized his observation point was a potential bomb, he moved quickly deeper into the city.

Desert Fire

The nearest rifle shots were only two blocks away when he took refuge in a building. Entry was made easy by the gaping hole in the large glass door. He stepped over the broken glass and searched the dark interior for signs of life. Satisfied the ground floor was deserted, he made his way to the stairs and climbed slowly upward.

The building was a modern four-storey structure with hundreds of square feet of glass windows adorning each level. Campbell remained in the stairwell until he reached the roof. He moved to the edge and peered out over the town. It appeared deserted. With the exception of the gunfire in the streets, nothing seemed alive.

A tank moved into his view, two blocks away and one street removed from the building upon which he perched. Campbell had the eerie feeling that he wasn't a part of the scene unfolding before him, but rather a ghost-like, interested-but-neutral, observer. The tank fired its main gun and Campbell felt the building rattle from the concussion as the large projectile sped towards a target in the city. The shell struck a building four blocks south of the tank and ripped a large chunk of concrete from the facing wall, pushing it inward and exploding it outward at the same time.

Another tank moved into view, next to the first. Suddenly one of the tanks seemed to explode. When the smoke cleared, it sat, a burning hulk, as the second tank moved away at top speed, small flames from the burning pieces of the destroyed tank lighting its upper surface. *How the hell did that happen? It's almost like there was a forward observer out here, calling in the shots.*

Campbell searched the tops of the nearby buildings, straining his eyes in the ghostly light cast by the falling illumination canisters. The small arms fire seemed to be fading to the south. *I can't believe the Allies are falling back. This is a nightmare. None of it's real.*

The soft crunch of a booted foot on broken glass brought

him back to his own building. He moved quietly to a position behind the stairwell entrance and waited. A head peeked cautiously from the stairwell doorway, followed by the rest of the body in a half crouch. The head and shoulders of a second man was visible when the first soldier saw Campbell and spun his rifle.

Campbell was a half-second ahead of his adversary. The rapid cyclic rate of his AK-47 sent bullets smashing first into one soldier, then the other, then the wall, as the two bodies were no longer there to absorb the impacts. The bolt slammed home on an empty chamber and came to rest. Campbell drew his knife and rushed forward, ready for the worst, but there was no need for haste. These two had no fight left in them; their lives lay in fast-forming pools oozing from their prone bodies.

Quickly, he stripped them of their weapons and ammunition and rushed down the stairs. At the broken door to the street, he paused only long enough to assure himself there was enough time to make a dash to the adjacent building in relative safety. He hit the sidewalk running and rounded the corner of the building at full speed, ducking into a broken door only thirty feet from the corner.

He held his breath, his back to the wall near the door, listening for the sounds of men on foot. When he was no longer able to restrict his body from needed oxygen, he sucked air into his lungs.

The metallic sound of an advancing tank rattled off the inside of the building. Campbell squatted and peeked out the door. A heavy artillery round exploded in the street only thirty yards from the fast-moving tank. Campbell ducked back inside as shrapnel and chunks of concrete and asphalt slammed into the building. *That can't be coincidence. That's two arty rounds almost dead center on target. Somebody has got to be calling that stuff in. But where the hell is he?*

He peeked into the street again and saw Iraqi soldiers on the flanks and to the rear of the tank. *Shit!* Small arms fire poured into the side of the building. What glass was left unbroken in the windows disintegrated around him. He crawled on his hands and knees toward the rear of the building, bullets whizzing overhead, his knees bleeding from cuts caused by the broken glass.

The front wall of the building disintegrated in a bright flash of light and a thundering explosion. Campbell was thrown over a desk and into the rear wall by the concussion. He fought for his breath and searched in the dusty darkness for his weapons, lost in the blast. He found one nearby and got to his feet, groaning involuntarily from the pain and exertion. He pulled the bolt to the rear and checked the action. It seemed to be functional.

He opened a door leading to an alley and stepped outside. Several troops came into view as they rounded the edge of the building and stepped into the alley. Campbell fired two short bursts. Two or three of them fell, the others ducking out of sight behind the building. Campbell ran toward the end of the alley opposite the soldiers. He heard the buzz of the bullets around him before he heard the reports from the automatic rifles. Slugs ricocheted off the walls around him and whined further into the darkness.

Campbell hit the end of the alley as three soldiers stepped into it at a dead run. He smashed one in the face with the butt of his rifle and fired, point-blank at the other two. He heard the bullets slap into their bodies and saw them fall with his peripheral vision as he continued around the corner of the building and down the sidewalk.

He ran close to the buildings on his side of the street, in blind desperation, not knowing where the enemy was, nor if his next step would be his last. His lungs burned like the exhausts on his F-18, and his legs began to shake; still he pressed on.

Campbell turned left a block, then right two, then left two then right two. He collapsed in a heap near the back door of an empty restaurant, his body shaking from fear and exertion, demanding that he go no further. His heart thumped against his chest in what surely must be a valiant attempt to escape its confines and leave this crazy man who would destroy it. Campbell hugged the AK-47 tightly under his armpit, his back to the wall of the restaurant.

"Psst! Hey, crazy man, you speak English?" A voice whispered loudly from the protection of the corner of the building.

Campbell spun in the direction of the voice, his hand on the trigger of the AK-47. "Who the hell wants to know? Hey, man, you an American?"

"Cominski. Recon Battalion. Now who the hell are you? Talk fast or we'll blow your fucking head off."

Campbell felt the flood of relief wash his body. "James Campbell. Captain. U.S.M.C. 525-55-1515. It's good to hear your voice, Cominski."

The voice remained behind the wall. "What the hell unit are you from? There's not anybody here from the Corps but our team."

"Goddamnit, Cominski, I'm a pilot. I was shot down the second day of the damn war. I've had a rough trip. You got a smoke?"

Cominski stepped around the corner. "Yep. You're a jughead."

Two other marines stepped out of the shadows from the opposite side of the street. All three rushed to him. One of the men who had held his silence during Cominski's brief interrogation said, "Good to see you, Captain. I'm Corporal Hodge and the tall lanky drink-of-water with me is PFC Oberlander. We don't have time to talk. Follow us. We've got a fairly secure position a couple of blocks away."

"Lead on, Corporal."

They moved cautiously south, no more than a block, and entered a five-story office building. Campbell felt his legs growing rubbery as they climbed the stairs to the roof, but pride wouldn't

Desert Fire

let him complain. Just as he was about to give up his pride, they stepped onto the roof. Three more marines were kneeling in positions on three sides of the building. Two PRC-25 field radios sat propped up against the stairwell wall.

"We got him, Spanky. Says he's a Captain in the Corps. I believe him. Hell, you should'a seen him shoot and run. Hot damn!" said Hodge. "And the first damn thing he asked for was a smoke."

"Not so loud, Pup." Spanky said as he walked in a crouch to the stairwell entrance. He put out his hand. "Corporal Louis Franklin. They call me Spanky."

Campbell shook his hand. "Captain Jim Campbell, but I'll be damned if you can't call me anything you want."

Spanky smiled, his bright teeth almost the only thing visible in the camouflage paint on his face. He pointed to the corners of the building. "That over there is PFC Riley, better known as Lugwrench. And the other one is PFC B.J. Smith, also known as Smitty. Welcome aboard, sir."

Campbell nodded to them, his movement made more visible by a fresh round of illumination. "You guys don't know how good it is to see you."

Hodge pulled out a pack of non-filter cigarettes and offered one to Campbell. "You'll have to step into the stairs to smoke it, sir."

Campbell snatched the cigarette and smiled. "I don't have anything but the habit. And don't call me 'sir' again. At least not out here. It's Jim. I hear Spanky call you Pup?"

Hodge fished for his lighter. "Yessir. I mean Captain Jim."

Campbell accepted the lighter and hesitated. He thought of Akbar. "A damn good gypsy fella in Iraq called me that."

"It just seemed to fit."

"Captain Jim it is then. Now if you gents will excuse me, I'm stepping into the smoking room." He stepped back into the stairwell.

Stoney Livingston

"You guys take your positions," ordered Spanky. He followed Campbell into the darkened stairwell.

Campbell cupped his lighter as he fired up the cigarette. The first drag sent him into a short coughing fit. When he regained control, he looked at Spanky. "Damn, that felt good." He motioned with his hand to the rooftop outside. "Are you in communication with any of our people?"

Spanky smiled. "We're the ones been calling in the arty. They can't figure out what in the hell is going on down there. We've nailed three of 'em for sure, maybe four."

Campbell took another drag and inhaled it slowly. "Yeah, you guys are doing a helluva job." He took another drag. "How far is the fire direction center? I've got to get there a.s.a.p. I've got intelligence for the brass."

There was a short silence. "Captain, I'm afraid that's gonna be a little tough right now."

"Why's that?"

"There are no friendlies in the city. Basically, we're surrounded."

CHAPTER 13

"Surrounded?" said Campbell quietly.

"I'm afraid so, sir."

"What the hell happened, Spanky? Where are the good guys? What's going on around here? How the hell could we be surrounded with all the ordinance we've got over here?"

"I don't know what happened, sir. I think the Saudis mistook the Iraqi units as ours. I'm not sure. Anyway, my team and Pup's were in the city on a recon. We saw the tanks rolling in and took up separate positions. I didn't know Pup and his men were still here until about twenty minutes ago. We hooked up on the air and rallied to this building.

"We've been looking for a way out, but right now, there isn't any."

"What do you hear on the radio? Does it sound like we're mounting a counter-offensive?"

"To be honest, sir, the only thing we can understand is the man they have in the FDC. We're calling in the shots and he's answering us in English. Most everything else we're hearing is Arabic."

Campbell fieldstripped his cigarette butt out of habit. "Sounds like we got 'em right where we want 'em, right?"

"Yessir. We can attack in any direction."

"I like your attitude, Spanky."

"Sir, why are you wearing those clothes? Lugwrench almost sniped you until he saw you shootin' at the Iraqis."

"It's a long story. I'll tell you about it over a beer someday."

"Not in this country. Hell, we're doing good to get anything as strong as soda pop."

"You ever been on an aircraft carrier?"

"No, sir."

"I'll see to it you all get aboard the *Coral Sea* when we get out of this shit. You'll get that beer then."

"Sounds like a grand plan to me, Captain."

Campbell said. "What's the plan for the rest of the night?"

"Well, sir, we figured on stayin' here and callin' 'em in until our batteries are dead. I was thinking of sending out a scout team to find a way outa here, but I'm not so sure. It's confusing as hell. There must be some resistance out there, 'cause the Iraqis keep shootin' at something, but we haven't seen a fuckin' thing."

"How much ammo have you got for the M-16s?"

"We've still got a full combat load. 'Cept for Lugwrench. He dropped a couple Iraqis a little earlier and hauled-ass. Some of them know we're here, but I don't think they know who we are or what we're doin'. Probably think we're a squad of grunts or somethin'."

"How secure is this building?"

Spanky smiled again. "If you hadn't come in with our guys, chances are you'd a been blown to hell. We've got charges set at the entrances. Nothing real big – we had to stretch our plastic – but enough to waste a man or two – give us advance warning without placing a man downstairs."

Campbell sighed. "Well, it's your show. What do you want me to do?"

"I don't know, sir. I don't know what the hell to do. If we wait for daylight and there's no counter-attack, we're as good as dead if they find us. But if we stay here, we can call in some pretty accurate fire on their armor."

"Your choice, Spanky. I'm just along for the ride."

"Thank you, sir." He paused. "If it's just the same to you, I'd like to stay here and call 'em in."

Campbell rubbed his hands together. "Let's do it." He stepped out onto the roof.

It was shortly after two-thirty in the morning when one of the charges on the ground floor exploded. Campbell was instantly awakened from a fitful sleep. He grabbed the AK-47 at his side and waited for Spanky to issue an order. He didn't have to wait long.

"Pup, take Lugwrench and Ski. Take a radio and keep me posted."

"You got it," answered Pup. Lugwrench was already in the stairwell, waiting, Ski right behind him. Pup picked up the radio and put it on his back and joined the men at the stairs.

"Hey, Spanky, you mind if I tag along with Pup?"

"This ain't like flyin' an airplane, sir."

Campbell knew there was little time to waste in discussion. "I'm ex Force Recon. I can handle it."

A look of respect spread across Spanky's face. He smiled. "Be my guest, Captain."

Campbell turned and followed Pup and his men down the stairs, quickly but quietly. As they neared the ground floor, the sound of a man moaning in pain reached them. There were no other noises. Cautiously, they entered the floor and spread out in the large office. Campbell stayed behind Ski, who had been silently assigned the duty of checking out the injured man.

The man lay with his back against a wall, his arms, face and chest bleeding profusely. He wiped his eyes as Ski stepped on a piece of broken glass and they grew large and round with fear as he saw the marine approaching him. He looked for his weapon, but before he could find it, Ski was on him. The man's efforts to resist were feeble and Ski quickly overpowered him. Campbell picked up the rifle the man had been searching for and knelt next to Ski and the wounded man.

Ski reached for a canteen. "We gotta clean him up. Hell, I can't even see where he's hit, there's so much blood." The Iraqi

171

soldier lay motionless, eyes open wide, unsure of their intent.

Campbell unsheathed his knife and cut a piece of cloth from the soldier's sleeve. He handed it to Ski.

Ski poured water onto the soldier's face and swiped at the diluted blood with the cloth. Several small lacerations became visible. "Shit. He's got a chunk of steel right below the left eyeball." Ski tried to pry it out with his dirty fingernail. The soldier screamed in agony. Ski jumped back. He looked at the Iraqi indignantly. "All right, Godamnit. I'll leave the fucking thing in there. But if you scream one more time, I'll cut your throat. You hear me?" He moved his index finger across his throat.

"Godamnit, keep him quiet over there." It was Pup.

Lugwrench was out of sight, somewhere on the backside of the building.

Ski replied, "I'm tryin'. Hell, he ain't hit that bad. We could've done a better job with those charges."

"Keep it down, Ski."

Ski turned back to the Iraqi. He looked up at Campbell. "Well, now that we got our very own fucking prisoner of war, what the hell are we gonna do with him?"

Campbell answered. "I'm not worried about him. We can drag him along with us, but I'm pretty sure he isn't alone. I'm a little worried we haven't heard from his pals yet."

A single shot rang out from the alley behind the building.

"Lugwrench! What the hell is going on back there?"

Silence followed. Campbell left Ski with the prisoner and moved to the rear of the building. The door to the alley was open. He moved to the side of the door and waited a few seconds, listening. Hearing nothing, he stepped into the alley in a low crouch, his rifle at the ready. In the darker shadow of the building across the street, he saw Lugwrench struggling with a lifeless form.

"Who's that?" asked Lugwrench.

"Jim Campbell."

Desert Fire

Campbell could hear the proud smile in Lugwrench's voice. "Well, howdy, Captain Jim. You wouldn't mind giving me a hand with this one would you?"

Campbell rushed across the narrow alley. "Is he still alive?"

"Don't think so, but he's got all kinda gear hangin' offa his ass. Must be some kind of officer or something. Can't do a real good search out here in the open. Makes me kinda nervous."

Campbell handed his rifle to Lugwrench. "I'll take him." He squatted down and Lugwrench leaned the body over his lowered shoulders. They crossed the alley and entered their command post. Campbell placed the body gently on the floor. The short trip across the alley was about all his body could handle in its current physical condition. He breathed heavily as Lugwrench conducted a thorough search of the body.

"This guy's no officer. But he *was* an FO." Lugwrench held up a map pouch so the light from the illumination rounds outside flickered on it. "Hell, I'll bet there's all kinds of good information here."

"Let me see it," said Campbell.

Lugwrench handed the canvas bag to him.

"Let me borrow your flashlight."

Lugwrench unsnapped the small flashlight from his utility blouse pocket and handed it to him. Campbell studied the three maps, closing his eyes after peering at each one. He put the maps in the bag and placed it on the floor. "What else you find?"

"A damn good pair of field glasses and a bunch of stuff written in a small notebook."

"Let me see the notebook."

Lugwrench handed him the book and Campbell made mental negatives of each page containing material. When he was done, he put the notebook in the map case and left it on the floor. When he looked up at Lugwrench, the man was staring at him.

"You know something, Captain Jim? I swear, you looked

just like you were takin' pictures of those pages, the way you were flippin' through 'em and blinkin' your eyes. You shoulda seen it. Weirdest thing I ever saw."

"No kidding? Must be the light."

"Yeah, probably so. You see anything interesting?"

"There was..."

"Here comes the first team!" shouted Pup. "Tanks! Two of 'em. And they've got infantry with 'em. It looks like they've made us. Let's get some firepower over here."

Lugwrench took a position near the door. Ski dragged the wounded soldier to a window facing the street. Pup was on the radio to the roof. Campbell took a position near him and aimed in on the troops near the advancing tanks.

Pup unkeyed the handset of the radio and hung it on its hook. "They'll be down in a second. Hold your fire until they get down, then fire two or three short burst and haul-ass out the back. I'll be at the back door and make sure it's secure." He moved to the alley side of the building.

"I'm not into this takin' on tanks with M-16s bullshit," said Ski.

"It's only diversionary. We give 'em a burst and get the hell outta here. It slows down the infantry. We can hide from the tanks if we can slow down the troops," said Campbell.

"Anything you say, Captain Jim." Ski aimed down his rifle barrel.

Spanky and his men came charging down the stairs. Ski opened up first. Lugwrench and Campbell were right behind him. Spanky and his men made it out the rear door.

"Let's get outa here!" shouted Campbell. As they hit the alley, the front of the building disintegrated, the shock waves sending dust and debris through the open door and the windows, into the alley, seeming to chase the retreating marines.

A squad of Iraqi infantry cut off their retreat. They held up at the corner of an office building.

Desert Fire

"Godamnit!" Spanky turned to Lugwrench. "Lugwrench, I need you and one more volunteer to create a diversion. Lead 'em northeast. Rally at four when you can. Pick your man."

"I'll go." Campbell heard his own voice. "Give me an M-16 and some ammo."

Ski offered his weapon. "I can't do much good with it while I'm babysittin' this P.O.W."

Campbell took the rifle and offered cartridge belt. He buckled the cartridge belt around his robe, looked over at Lugwrench and said, "You ready?"

Lugwrench spat onto the sidewalk. "I don't get no readier, Cap'n Jim. Let's haul-ass."

"You lead."

"You're doin' just fine for a wing wiper. It's your show, sir."

Bullets from the advancing squad ricocheted off the surrounding walls. "Let's go!" Campbell broke into a dead run.

"Whoa! Goddamn! Not that way! We skirt 'em first."

Campbell heard the words, but it was too late. He was committed to a direct route northeast. He fired a burst from the M-16. Having gotten used to the heavier recoil of the AK-47, he found the M-16 much easier to handle than before his experience with the heavier-caliber communist-made weapon. His accuracy on the run was deadly. The enemy troops withdrew to cover. He heard Lugwrench on his heels.

He rounded a corner and circled back toward the Iraqis. Lugwrench caught up to him and tugged on his sleeve. "Where the hell you goin', sir?"

Campbell slowed to a walk. "I thought we'd circle around 'em and hit 'em once on the flank. Make 'em think there was more of us out here than there really are."

"Beggin' your pardon, sir, but that's crazy. You been flyin' fighters too long. All we got is these rifles."

Campbell stopped. "Where is rally point four?"

"It's on the southern edge of town. Big department store.

Painted a bright yellow. Can't miss the damn thing, even if we didn't have the illumination."

"I'll tell you what. You draw their fire directly to the northeast and I'll hit 'em on the flank. I'll meet you at the rally point."

"That sounds shaky as hell to me, sir. Spanky didn't say anything about attacking from the flank."

Campbell gave up the fight. "Okay, Lugwrench. You win. Let's back up and hit 'em from the front, then run like hell."

Lugwrench smiled. "You damn near had me convinced you were crazy enough to flank the bastards."

They turned and made for the last position of contact. The strength of numbers made the Iraqis less careful than the Americans and Campbell heard them before he saw them. He and Lugwrench waited on opposite sides of the street as the Iraqis advanced carelessly down the center of the street. *I can't believe this shit. They must think they're on parade.* He opened up with his M-16. He heard the other M-16 join his in a song of death. In seconds, the street was empty, save five dead or wounded soldiers, laying on the asphalt. The others had taken cover without firing a shot,

Campbell stuck a fresh magazine in his rifle. He looked across the street to where Lugwrench stood in the dark shadow cast by the illumination rounds still going off overhead. He saw Lugwrench give him the thumbs up sign. They advanced down the street, hugging the sides of the buildings.

A sound off to his left caught Campbell's attention. He turned and fired at a piece of uniform disappearing deeper into the shadows. He heard the clatter of a weapon falling, then a groan.

The sounds of men running – canteens bouncing against bayonet scabbards, gear rattling – reached Campbell. It seemed less than a block away. He motioned to Lugwrench who quickly joined him.

"I heard 'em," said Lugwrench. "Here come the Indians."

Desert Fire

Campbell smiled at the trite American joke. "Let's draw 'em northeast."

"I'm with you."

The first two men of the advancing Iraqi unit came into view, followed by a tank. The marines fired short bursts from their rifles and beat a hasty retreat northeast. The small arms fire around the city had died down to sporadic exchanges in the central part of the city. Campbell wondered if Spanky and his men were okay.

Campbell sat with his back to the wall extending two and a half feet above the top of the roof. He smoked a cigarette as the sun peaked over the horizon. It had been a long night but, after they ran from the tank, they had not exchanged fire with the Iraqis. They had fired a few bursts into the air to draw attention to themselves, but nothing resembling another confrontation developed. It had taken them two hours to get to the rally point.

Spanky sat next to him. "Too bad we lost those maps. They might have told us something."

Campbell exhaled a cloud of smoke. "Yeah. I think I can remember some of it though."

"Lugwrench says you're a good hand with that M-16."

"He don't do so bad himself."

Spanky smiled. "He's our sniper."

Ski crawled next to them. "There's two tanks in the street below us. About a block east. You want we should call in a mission?"

Spanky sighed. "We got any battery left?"

Ski nodded. "Pup's radio is still puttin' out."

"Go ahead, but start the bracket away from us. After what we been through, there's no sense gettin' blown away by our own side."

Ski crawled to Pup who slept by his radio. Lugwrench was curled up in the fetal position only a few feet away.

Stoney Livingston

The illumination stopped. The sky was grey and dismal; not a sound pierced the air for several moments. "Kinda weird, ain't it?"

Campbell looked at Spanky. "Yeah. I don't know how those guys in World War Two, Korea and Vietnam took it so long. It's like a big dream. More like a nightmare. Can you imagine going through this shit every day for a year or more?"

"Not without a beer now and then."

Campbell shook his head and smiled a wistful smile. "Funny, the things that are important to different people at different times."

The two fell silent and stared at the brightening sky. After a while, Spanky said, "If the coalition don't make a push, we're in big trouble."

"Did you get an idea of their strength?"

Spanky shook his head. "Not for sure. From what I saw, it looked like at least regimental size, but I think we only saw a small part of it. I'm guessing there's at least a division out there."

Campbell nodded. "I think you're right."

The heavy whish of an artillery round passed overhead. Campbell heard the explosion in the streets below and watched almost disinterestedly as Ski called in a correction. "How long you been in, Spanky?"

"Four years in April."

"Stayin'?"

Spanky shook his head. "Naw. When this one's over, I'm outa here. One war is enough for me."

Campbell thought of Wyman. "Yeah, it is for most people. I've got a buddy in my squadron who flew A-4s in Vietnam. He's got four confirmed kills. I think the only reason he stayed in all these years was to get that fifth one. I hope he gets it and gets the hell out. He's a helluva guy."

"What about you, Captain? You stayin' in?"

Another round flew overhead. Campbell waited until it

exploded below them. "No, I don't think so. I think I'll get out and look for a nice quiet desk job somewhere. Maybe I'll dig ditches. I don't know. Can't figure out why I stayed in this long. I guess it's because I couldn't afford my own plane that puts out the thrust an F-18 does."

"You fly F-18s?"

"Did."

Spanky had a look of excitement on his face. "Shit, man, that F-18 is one bad airplane!"

"We were mostly looking to engage Iraqi aircraft, but the Iraqis haven't been too cooperative about that. I'm not so sure Saddam Hussein has a real air force. We sure haven't seen much of it if he does."

Two more artillery rounds raced to the target, exploding almost as one. Ski turned around and smiled from ear to ear. "One of them puppies just blew the hell outa an Iraqi soup can."

Pup yawned himself awake and took over the radio. Oberlander and Smitty brewed ration coffee over a heat tab.

"Hey, Obie, the smell of that coffee will draw those Arabs here like shit draws flies," said Spanky. "Kill it."

Reluctantly, Oberlander picked up the can of water and smothered the heat tab. "Damnit, Spanky, those fucking Arabs are pissin' me off. I don't mind fightin' a war now and then, but by gawd, a man oughta be able to have a cup of coffee in the morning."

"I hate to agree with Obie on anything, but he's right on that one," said Smitty. "Why don't we just go down there and kick some ass so we can have our coffee?"

"There's something goin' on," said Pup, his ear to the handset. "There's all kinds of shit on the air, and most of it is Arabic."

Campbell, Smitty and Obie moved to the perimeter of the building while Spanky sat next to the radio and listened intently, trying to pick out any transmissions in English. Campbell stared out over the city of Khafji. Except for a few damaged buildings, it looked like a city in the aftermath of an orderly evacuation. It brought to mind images of an old television show called *The Twilight Zone*.

He could see no movement below. The burning hulk of an Iraqi tank sent small wisps of pitch-black smoke curling skyward. The crew was nowhere to be seen, nor was the other tank that had been with it only moments before.

Campbell looked south and saw the faint signs of dust that drifted into the sky, announcing the arrival of a mechanized army. Even on paved roads, the telltale dust was there. The tracked vehicles, especially, sent up the signal, long after leaving the sand and dirt.

Campbell moved next to the radio. He tapped Spanky on the shoulder. "We've got something moving in our direction from the south. Can't tell what it is yet, but it appears to be a pretty large unit."

"Roger." He turned to Lugwrench. "Lug, take up a position on the south wall with Captain Jim."

Lugwrench nodded and complied with the order silently. Campbell moved to the west end of the wall and waited, his hands gripping the M-16.

"It's Iraqis!" said Lugwrench. His vantagepoint put him at a better angle to view the advance than did Campbell's.

Campbell moved next to him. He looked at the advancing column, then glanced over his shoulder to Spanky. "I think you were right about that division. And I think the whole damn thing is headed our way right now."

CHAPTER 14

Spanky picked up the handset. "We've gotta break in. I just wish I knew what in the hell they were sayin'." He keyed up the mike.

Campbell turned his attention back to the advancing column. *This rooftop doesn't look like the place to be to me. We ought to get back down to the street and try to skirt around them and head south. They must be retreating.*

The lead elements of the column were within five hundred yards when the second vehicle in line exploded. The bright orange flash and the ensuing cloud of black smoke were followed by the sound of the explosion, then the whish of the round before it struck the target. *Odd, how that happens. Those guys are already dead, then I hear the explosion, then I step back further in time and I hear the round before it's even hit the target and exploded. Too bad I can't stop time at that last sound, kind of turn everything around, stop this whole damn war.*

He heard muffled shouts of glee behind him as Spanky and Pup whooped it up. "Nice shootin'," he heard Pup say. "The first one was right on target. Now that's one to write home about."

The column broke left and right and sped pass the burning tank. Other vehicles to the rear left the column and took side streets in what appeared to Campbell a haphazard fashion. Spanky continued to call in fire missions. Saudi and American artillery poured into the streets. The Iraqis were in a rout. There was no order or coordination below them. It was every man for himself.

An APC slammed into a building as it tried to negotiate a

turn too fast. The troops inside flowed out onto the street and ran madly north on foot, passing within a few feet of the department store upon which the marines perched. The driver of the vehicle managed to disentangle it from the damaged wall of the building and drove north, on the heels of the frightened soldiers.

Artillery shells continued to rain on the city and hundreds of Iraqi troops passed the marine position as the day wore on, but the Allied infantry did not appear. It was almost noon when the marines were spotted by an Iraqi tank crew.

Lugwrench peered over the top of the short retaining wall and said, "Shit! There's a tank down there zeroing in on us." He dove to the deck and crawled for the north end of the roof as fast as his body could propel him in that posture. Campbell was right behind him.

The 135mm projectile struck the south wall only five feet below the roof line. Concrete and drywall shot skyward. The explosion was deafening. Campbell covered his head with his arms as debris fell back onto the roof. In the heavy cloud of dust, he heard Spanky's voice.

"Give me a casualty report!"

"Ski here."

"Lug. I'm okay"

"Pup. Check."

"Obie. I'm still in one piece, I think."

"Smitty. Okay, but that sonafabitch pissed me off real good."

"Campbell here."

"With that tank on our ass, we haven't got a chance. Let's make like a sheepherder and get the flock outa here," said Obie.

"Pup, we got any explosive left?" asked Spanky.

Pup looked at him in the clearing cloud of dust. "Not enough to do any fucking good against a tank."

They were all against the north retaining wall. Smitty pulled out a pack of cigarettes and offered one to Campbell, who took it with a smile. Smitty leaned his head up against the wall. "What the hell you gonna do? Get a cancer?"

A second round slammed into the building. Part of the roof collapsed onto the floor below.

"Godamnit, Spanky, we gotta do something," said Pup.

"We only got three choices: sit it out, run like hell, or send a team after that tank."

"Fuck three choices. I say we got one, and that's run like hell," said Obie.

Campbell took a hurried drag from his smoke. "Sounds like the best plan to me, Spanky. Unless you got something specific lined up."

Spanky looked at his team. "Let's get the hell outa here."

A third shell hit the building, collapsing most of what was left of the roof, sending two of the men to the floor below with the debris. The others hung on to the retaining wall.

"Who the hell's missing?" asked Spanky.

"Lugwrench and Obie," answered Campbell. "I saw 'em fall."

The gaping hole in the roof exposed the floor below, but the settling dust made clear observation impossible. Spanky said, "Let's find a way down there. One more shot and we're dead."

"Over here! There's a beam laying at an angle. I think we can make it," said Pup.

They crawled to the beam and quickly and easily negotiated the descent to the floor below. Once on the floor, they called for the two missing men. They heard Obie first. He was half buried in a pile of debris. They pulled him out, bruised but otherwise unhurt.

Another shell struck the south wall. What was left of the roof crashed to the floor below, missing the marines who stood under the exposed sky. Campbell and Ski watched the stairs and hall while the others continued their search for Lugwrench.

"Godamn, Spanky, we'll never find him in all of this shit.

Let's a couple of us draw that tank away. Give the rest of us time to search for Lugwrench."

In the stairwell, Campbell saw a rifle barrel then a soldier's arm. When the upper shoulder came into view, Campbell fired a burst from his M-16. The enemy rifle fell onto the floor at the curve in the stairwell. The soldier fell backward, down the stairs. Campbell could tell by the sounds of rifle barrels banging into one another, there were others behind his victim who were making their way up the stairs.

Spanky was at his side. "We're in deep shit. Here. Hold 'em off. We haven't found Lugwrench yet." He handed Campbell four hand grenades.

"What? No instructions?" Campbell smiled.

"Fake it." Spanky grinned as he rushed back into the interior of the room to continue his search.

Campbell heard movement below. He pulled the pin on one of the grenades and held the spoon as he took three steps down the stairs. He released the pin and held the grenade to the count of two, then tossed it gently around the wall to the lower level. He barely made the three steps back up to the next floor when the grenade exploded. The blast was followed by several screams, then moaning.

"I found him!" shouted Smitty. "Give me a hand here."

Campbell heard the sounds of heavy objects crashing in the room behind him as the marines cleared the debris from Lugwrench. Shortly, there was silence, then Spanky approached him in a fast crouch. "He's alive, but he's got a broken leg, and he's been unconscious. He's coming around now."

Another 135mm round slammed into the building. Suddenly, the marines found themselves on what was now the roof. The floor above them was completely gone. "Is everybody okay?" asked Spanky.

Campbell's ears rang loudly. "Campbell here," he answered. The ringing was so loud, he couldn't be sure how many of the others answered. Then he heard Pup's voice.

"Looks like we made it one more time."

Smitty looked up at the clear sky overhead. "I've never been in a convertible building before. Think they could do this to my old Chevy?"

"Cut the crap, Smitty. We gotta figure a way outa here," said Spanky, unable to completely hold back his smile.

Ski shouted from his position at the end of the hall. "They're bringin' in the first team. We got a squad with a rocket launcher comin' in the ground floor now."

Spanky looked to Campbell, then to Pup. "Pup, it's you or Captain Jim. Take the guys and try to fight your way outa here. I'm staying with Lugwrench. The bone is sticking out his leg. If we move him, we might puncture the femoral artery."

Pup looked quickly at Campbell. "It's your show, Captain Jim. If you don't mind, I'll stay here with Spanky and kick Iraqi ass."

"Hey, who said I was going anywhere?" asked Smitty. "We all came into this shit together. I'll pick my own friends, thank you." He glanced at Campbell. "No offense, Captain Jim, but I came in here with Lugwrench. If he stays, so do I."

Campbell nodded silently.

"I don't feel like a whole lot of running around myself," said Obie.

"Who's bullshittin' who? Ain't none of us goin' anywhere, unless Lug makes the trip."

Campbell looked at each man quickly. They were an unlikely family, but he had never seen stronger ties. He shrugged. "No sense me running out just when the party's starting to warm up."

Smiles all around greeted him.

"If we're gonna make a stand here, against a division or so, I've got to use the radio. You got a code book?" said Campbell.

Spanky shook his head.

Pup looked at him sadly. "The only radio that had any battery left is probably in orbit now. The tank got it two shots ago."

"Great." *I've got to get that information to the Allies.*

Lugwrench was fully conscious, his face twisted in pain. He looked up at Spanky and said through clenched teeth, "That whole goddamn roof musta fallen on me, huh? Oh! God! It hurts."

"Hold still Goddamnit, Lug. You want some morphine?"

His brow and upper lip were drenched in perspiration. He nodded. "I hate to cop out on you, Spanky, but I'm afraid – Ah! I'm afraid I need it."

Pup moved in with the needle and syringe.

"I hear the bastards. They're just below us. If they get the angle and put a rocket through the floor, we're dead meat," said Ski.

Campbell pulled the pin on a grenade and held the spoon in place. He picked up his M-16 and looked at Ski and Smitty. "You guys wanna kick some ass?"

Ski checked the magazine in his rifle and inserted a fresh one. Smitty nodded.

"Let's go." Campbell charged down the stairs, Ski and Smitty right behind him. As he turned the corner to the next landing, he released the spoon on the grenade and let it fly. He tossed it as hard as he could onto the lower deck and watched it bounce out of sight. The walls shook with the concussion in the enclosed area, and Campbell lead the charge into the room, the trigger on his M-16 held back.

The noise was deafening, but paled by comparison to the confusion among the Iraqi soldiers. The room seemed filled with bodies, all of them moving in different directions. When his magazine was empty, Campbell quickly replaced it with a full one, but there was no one left standing to shoot. The three marines quickly checked the fallen men, throwing weapons out of reach of all of them.

Campbell ran to the stairs and pulled the pin on another grenade. He looked over his shoulder. "You guys ready for another round?"

Smitty shrugged. "Why not? Shit, this is fun."

Ski said, "Count me in."

Campbell charged down the stairs. He tossed the grenade, waited for the explosion, then bolted onto the next floor.

There was no one – dead or alive. The floor appeared empty. This was the first floor dedicated to the display of merchandise, the top two being used primarily for warehousing. They moved among the aisles and behind the counters, searching for the Iraqis, certain that at any moment they would all jump out of hiding and open fire.

The only sounds were those of booted feet striking the carpet. The sound of a low-flying jet passed over them. All three were on the floor instantly at the sound. Campbell was the first to regain his feet.

"Goddamn, Captain, get down until we know who the hell those planes belong to," said Smitty.

"That was the sweet sound of an A-4 Skyhawk, gents. Get off your asses. Let's give 'em some support."

Pup appeared on the stairs behind them. "It's the Free Kuwaiti and the Saudi air forces. There are Saudi troops pouring into the city. Looks like we finally got into this war."

"No sense rushing into things," said Smitty evenly.

"Now, all we gotta do is let them know whose side we're on before they waste us," said Ski. "How about a white flag?"

Smitty shrugged. "Don't look at me. They didn't issue me no fucking white flag when I got outa boot camp."

"Skivvies," said Campbell.

Smitty turned to him. "Skivvies? We don't even have white skivvies. Jesus. I hadn't thought of that. That fucking brass don't want us to surrender at any cost."

"The Iraqis," said Campbell. "Some of them are bound to have white underclothes. Not many of 'em on that next floor," He nodded to the floor above, "will really care a whole lot if we borrow their skivvies."

Pup smiled. "That's real poetic, Cap'n Jim. Real poetic." He rushed to the floor above, followed closely by Campbell and Smitty.

They stripped five of the dead before finding a piece of white cloth large enough to display as a white flag. It was an undershirt of sorts but most of it was bloody. By folding the dry portion around the outside of the bloody sections and tying it tight at the corners, they made a dirty white flag.

Spanky said, "Tie it to a rifle barrel and hand it to me."

Obie said, "Better you than me, oh fearless one. What if the Saudis don't feel like taking prisoners?"

Spanky shrugged. "Then I guess the rest of you will have to take on about a billion troops without me."

From behind the shelter of a remaining wall section, Smitty shouted. "Here they come! Looks like they're a little more organized than that mob that just left but that don't mean they're gonna take time to pay attention to a white flag."

Spanky had just finished tying the flag to a rifle barrel. Campbell snatched the rifle and said, "Give me your helmet."

Spanky looked at him dumbly. "What?"

"I said give me your helmet, corporal. That's an order."

"But..."

Campbell reached out and took the helmet from Spanky's head. "I think it'll be safer if I'm wearing this than nothing at all."

"But..."

"No buts, corporal. This is *my* job. You guys have done enough for today." He stuffed the helmet onto his head. "Give me your jacket."

Spanky hesitated.

"Damnit, Corporal, we're running out of time."

Desert Fire

Spanky removed his Jacket and handed it to Campbell. "This is bullshit, you know, Sir."

Campbell smiled at him and said, "Yeah, I know." He slipped the jacket over his robe and moved quickly to the stairwell and down to street level, listening to Spanky's verbal protests.

"It'd serve your right if you got your ass blown off, ya damn hero." The sound of Spanky's voice faded with the increase in distance between them.

CHAPTER 15

Campbell stopped near what was left of the front door to the building. There was just enough wall to hide him from the advancing troops, the foremost of which were about a block away. His mouth became unbearably dry as he waited for them to draw nearer. They appeared to be moving with just enough stealth to be able to hear him if he waited another five or six seconds before making his presence known.

Suddenly, at the end of the street away from the advancing Saudi forces, a light machine gun opened up with a long burst. Two or three of the Saudis fell. Campbell couldn't tell if they were dead or wounded or merely seeking cover.

"Damn!" he muttered. His position was between the opposing forces. This would probably not be a good time to offer the flag of surrender or truce. He moved away from the wall and into the interior of the building. He found a spot behind a mannequin, took off Spanky's helmet and field jacket, placed them on the store dummy, and moved behind a counter opposite the stairwell. He figured anyone entering the building would look to the stairwell first, away from his direction.

Outside, the sounds of battle raged incessantly. Campbell wondered if either side carried enough ammunition to maintain that rate of fire for any length of time. He felt certain Spanky and his men were ready for the worst only one floor above him. He wished there was something he could do to help them but the way things looked, there was little he could do to help himself. Occasionally, stray rounds entered his sanctuary and bounced from wall to wall before losing energy and coming to rest in a counter or other fixed object.

Desert Fire

Campbell doubted he could tell the difference between the Saudis and the Iraqis in a sudden encounter and that worried him. He didn't want to surrender to the wrong side and he damn sure didn't want to kill anybody on his side. He considered trying for the stairwell and taking his chances with the Marines above him but that probably wouldn't be such a good idea. They would probably kill the first thing that moved on that stairwell and, if he shouted to them to tell them who he was, somebody outside would hear him and there would be a three-way battle, most likely with the Saudis and Iraqis, both, shooting at the Marines.

Major Robert "Bob" "Pappy" Wyman eased back on the throttle and put his F-18 into a gentle dive. The search for the Iraqi Air Force was no longer his unit's priority. Today their aircraft were in air-to-ground configuration. Their mission was to support the coalition troops as they moved against Saddam Hussein's army. *It's about damned time*, he thought as he slowed his plane further to allow more time on target.

I wonder where Jim is? Is he down there? What if one of my missiles hits him? Wyman felt perspiration forming in the palm of his right hand. He could see the opposing forces below, each in a ragged line, winding through the city streets opposite one another. One of the buildings was missing a roof. It was as though someone had taken a large can opener and removed it. There appeared to be several figures near the windows on the exposed floor. Wyman couldn't be sure whose side they were on. He keyed up his air-to-air radio. "Dusty Red. See the building with the missing roof? Do not fire. I say again, do not fire. Let's make a pass to determine whose side those guys are on. Keep your eyes peeled. Break right and re-form and let me know what you think. From what I can see, they could be from either side. Dusty Red Three, go ground and try to find somebody who speaks English and find out what you can."

Posner answered, "Dusty Red Three, going ground

frequency. Will advise."

Wyman held his F-18 back, approaching dangerously close to stall speed. The F-18 was never designed to hover but Wyman knew this was as close to it as he would ever get.

"Pappy, we're closing in on you. You might want to pick it up. That's not a helicopter you're flying."

Redd's voice pulled Wyman from his concentrated stare at the troops in the building. He throttled up just before his aircraft lost lift and flew ten feet above the top edge of the building at a rapidly increasing speed. Small arms fire from the Iraqis in front of him poured his way in a steady stream. He banked right and flew toward the friendly forces behind him amid the brightly glowing tracers that outlined his craft.

"Damn, Pappy! What were you trying to do, read the rank on their uniforms?" Redd's voice gave away more than a little concern.

"They're U.S. Marines!" said Wyman.

"I think you're right, Pappy." It was Posner. He had apparently picked up something from ground radio. "There is a squad of grunts out here somewhere – an F.O. team. They were cut off yesterday and have been calling in artillery since then. Fire direction center lost contact a little while ago. Not known if their radio batteries went dead or if they were casualties."

"Roger that. Try to get ground location of friendlies. Let's give it another go and see what we can come up with."

Campbell watched, mesmerized, as his own squadron made its pass. Pappy was in the lead and trying to use his F-18 as a helicopter. He wondered what his flight leader was thinking. Not only was the F-18 not designed to fly that slow, it made an easy target when doing so. He wanted to warn them but he had no way of doing it without committing suicide. He wasn't yet ready for that move.

When the Marine F-18s rolled back for another pass,

Desert Fire

Campbell assumed that Pappy was ready to die, for he came in slowly, as before, but this time the planes were spread out, on line.

Suddenly, white flashes appeared from under the wings of the F-18s. Campbell dove for cover. The rockets sailed overhead and exploded amid the fleeing Iraqis. The coalition forces moved forward, firing constantly, not appearing to search for a target, rather, simply putting as much lead in the air as they possibly could in as short a time as possible. The noise was deafening.

Spanky and his men came down the stairwell, Lugwrench carried by two of them.

"That top floor was gettin' too damned hot," shouted Spanky as his men spread out to cover approaches to the building. "What the hell do we do now?"

Campbell said, "I'm displaying the white flag. If we wait any longer, it'll be too late."

"Better you than me, sir," came Spanky's quick reply.

A stray bullet ricocheted off of one of the concrete walls. It was followed almost immediately by several more. In an instant the interior of the building was deluged with hundreds of rounds, bouncing from wall to wall. The only thing the marines could do to protect themselves was to fall to the floor, which they did, almost in unison. A drill team would have had to practice hours to achieve such coordinated movement.

With his cheek pressed to the floor and his face turned toward Campbell, Smitty said, "I'm not real happy with this situation, Sir."

Despite their predicament, Campbell smiled. These men were facing almost certain death and yet they didn't give up. They still had a smart quip left.

Campbell crawled to the wall facing the street and stuck the barrel of his M-16, complete with dirty white flag, through an opening. "Hold your fire! Cease Fire! We are Americans! Cease

Fire!"

There was a sudden burst of fire in his direction, then it slowed to a stop.

"Cease Fire! We are Americans!" repeated Campbell.

A masculine voice replied, "How do we know this?"

Spanky answered, "If you'll stop all that damn shootin' for a minute, we'll show you."

The same masculine voice shouted a command in Arabic and there was silence in the immediate area. "Come out! No weapons!"

Campbell looked at Spanky, then to Smitty. "Me and you, Smitty. The rest of you stay put. If we convince 'em we are who we are without gettin' our heads blown off, we'll send for you."

Spanky started to protest. "But, Captain Jim..."

"No Buts. C'mon, Smitty. Let's get this done."

Smitty said, "When this is all over, I want a transfer to a different outfit." He stood and followed closely behind Campbell as the latter leaned his rifle, white flag and all, against the wall and stepped outside the shattered building.

Chapter 16

As they approached the man who appeared to be in charge of the coalition troops, Smitty said, "I feel naked without my rifle. Jesus! Look at all of 'em. Looks like they're all ready to mow us down. You sure this is a good idea?"

"Too late to change our minds now. We'd never make it to cover," replied Campbell quietly as he drew nearer the line of soldiers.

"Halt!" shouted the man in charge. Campbell could see now that he was a captain. He and Smitty came to an abrupt stop. They waited nervously while two of the men moved forward and checked them for weapons. The soldier who frisked Campbell grinned at him as he removed the knife from his robe.

When the two soldiers had returned to their formation, the captain stepped forward. "Give your names please," he said.

"I'm Captain James Campbell, United States Marine Corps. I'm a pilot. I was shot down on the second day of the war. The man with me is PFC B.J. Smith. He's a member of an F.O. team that's been calling in missions to make your life a little easier."

The captain said, "You wait. We have English speaker soon. You have others with?"

Campbell nodded. "They're behind me."

"You tell them come here now."

Campbell considered the order for a moment, studying the eyes of the man before him. Smitty looked at him questioningly. Campbell said, "They are American Marines. I'll ask them to come here but they will keep their weapons."

Stoney Livingston

"No! No keep weapons," said the captain.

Campbell smiled nervously, "Then I guess they'll stay where they are until we get an English speaker."

The captains eyes narrowed. "They come now!"

Campbell said, "Captain, we're on the same side. You won't disarm my men in a combat zone."

"How do I know this?"

"Because I wouldn't be stupid enough to show myself to you and pretend to be an American. That's spying."

"Not understand. You wait."

He and Smitty stood motionless for several moments until two American Marines arrived, one a sergeant, the other a lieutenant. They both ignored the coalition captain and stopped in front of Campbell. The lieutenant said, "Captain Campbell?"

"At your service, Lieutenant."

The lieutenant smiled and offered his hand. "Lieutenant David Briscoe, S2. We weren't certain you were still alive."

Campbell shook his hand. "I am. I assure you."

The sergeant stepped forward and shook Campbell's hand. "I'm Sergeant Williston. Proud to meet you, sir."

Campbell shook the sergeant's hand and introduced Smitty. "This is PFC Smith but we call him Smitty. He's part of an FO team that's been calling in arty for you guys. The rest of the team is in that building behind me." Smitty shook hands with the two.

Campbell glanced at the Coalition Captain then looked back at Briscoe. "Would you explain to this guy that we're on his side and the guys in the FO team aren't about to surrender their weapons after what they've just been through."

Sergeant Williston turned to the Captain and spoke in what appeared to Campbell to be fluent Arabic. When he finished, the Captain turned to his men and spoke briefly. All tension was gone. Campbell could see the smiles and relaxed postures.

Campbell said, "Is it okay to bring the FO team out?"

Briscoe smiled broadly. "You bet your ass. I'd like to meet these guys. When their radio went dead, we thought they'd bought the farm."

Campbell turned to face the building behind him. "Spanky. It's okay. Bring the squad down here. And don't forget our rifles."

"Roger," came the feint reply.

Campbell turned to Briscoe. "I've got intell. How do I get it to the brass?"

"You can accompany Sergeant Williston and me back to the command post."

"I'll wait for the FO team, if it's all right with you. They should be here in a minute."

"Not a problem, Captain," smiled Briscoe.

Spanky came into view first, cautiously, followed by the others, who were no less cautious. When he was next to Campbell, he handed the M-16 to him and hugged him. "We did it, Sir." Campbell hugged him back.

"We sure as hell did." He looked behind Spanky to see Obie and Ski, carrying Lugwrench. He turned to Lieutenant Briscoe. "Have we got a real stretcher? That man has a severely broken leg."

Sergeant Williston said, "We'll do better than that. I'll have an ambulance here in five minutes, Sir." He turned to the coalition captain and spoke rapidly.

After the coalition captain radioed his request for an ambulance, he ordered his men to move out. They disappeared when they turned left two blocks away from Campbell and his men.

CHAPTER 17

Campbell sat in the flight officer's office aboard the *U.S.S Coral Sea.* Lieutenant Colonel Robert Prescott, his wing commander, sat stiffly opposite him behind a grey desk. Prescott was okay as far as colonels went. He was a little stuffy for Campbell's tastes, but he had always seemed a fair man, and what more could you really ask of a man than that?

For two days, Campbell had undergone interrogation and re-introduction to the Marine Corps. He passed his information to G-2, the intelligence arm of the military, including details of the maps found on the Iraqi FO. Finally, he was allowed to report back to his unit aboard the *U.S.S. Coral Sea.* He could hardly wait to see Bob and the rest of the men in his squadron, but first, he had this unpleasant task before him.

Prescott cleared his throat. "I understand you've been through one hell of an ordeal, Jim." Prescott's eyes wavered momentarily but he regained control. He leaned across his desk. "Look, Jim, I'm no fucking psychiatrist. I don't know how to handle this kind of shit. I thought you had been thoroughly debriefed by all the Goddamn experts.

"I know you and I haven't always seen eye to eye on everything that's come up, but by gawd, we're both marines, and we know where the bear shit in the buckwheat. And what I'm trying to say is that you getting out of fighters isn't going to change the way wars are fought."

"It'll change the way *I* fight 'em."

"You know it will take a while to cut the papers and certify you for another aircraft. Jesus Christ, man, you're an F-18 pilot.

"Take a few days leave and get it together. If you still want out of F-18s when you get back, I won't stand in your way."

Desert Fire

"Thank you, sir. I appreciate your honesty. Believe me. I'd like to see Bob and the rest of the men in the squadron, then I'll talk to you about the leave."

"Did you hear that Bob got number five?"

Campbell jumped to his feet. "No shit?" He looked at Prescott with an embarrassed smile on his face. "I'm sorry, sir. It's just that I know Bob's waited almost twenty years for that to happen."

Prescott smiled a warm and genuine smile. "I think a lot of us wanted it almost as much as he did. Do you know that we have the only active flying ace in the Marine Corps?" He beamed proudly, as though he were talking about himself.

Campbell couldn't contain his excitement. "Can I see him now, sir?"

Prescott nodded. "Let me know about your leave request in the morning."

Campbell stood stiffly to attention. "Yessir. Will that be all, sir?"

"Dismissed, Captain."

Campbell did a picture-perfect about-face and marched from the cabin.

There was only one man in the officer's quarters when Campbell stepped in. He was an enlisted man, swabbing the deck. "Hey, sailor, where is everybody?"

The young seaman shot him a salty look. "They're all in the officer's mess, Captain. Some kind of party for Major Wyman. He's the only active ace in the Corps right now, you know."

Damn, even the navy says it with pride. "Thanks." Campbell spun about and charged to the officer's mess. When he walked through the hatch, the room looked deserted. He felt disappointment creep up on him. *Damn! I even miss the party Bob's been waiting for, for twenty years.*

A chorus of voices erupted into the Marine Corps Hymm. Men marched out of the kitchen in a column of twos, the lead pair carrying a large cake.

"From the halls of Montezuma to the shores of Tripoli.
We will fight our county's battles in the air, on land and sea.
First we fight for right and freedom. . . "

"What the hell's goin' on here?"

They continued to sing. *". . .then to keep our honor clean."*

"Hey. Hey, what's going on?"

The singing died out amid cheers and applause. The cake was placed in the center of a table. Ed Townsend approached and hugged him tightly. "I thought you were a goner. It's good to see you, Jim"

"Same here. The ragheads told me they got you."

Posner walked up to him. "Welcome back, Jim." He turned and faced the door. "And may I present our guest speaker, the world renowned ace fighter pilot, a living legend, the number two hot dog in Uncle Sam's Marine Corps, the one and only – Major Pappy Wyman!"

More applause and loud cheers. Wyman walked through the swinging stainless steel doors. Campbell moved to shake hands, but Wyman waved him back and stopped just outside the doors. "Gentlemen, we are gathered together here to pay tribute to one of the greatest heroes of modern warfare."

He was interrupted by cheers and cat-calls, whistles and shouts. He raised his hands. The room fell silent. "Please, gentlemen. Please." He kept his face straight. "We have among us now, the very man who discovered one of the world's best-kept secrets, and, while a prisoner of war, revealed it to the free world under the very noses – nay, at the request of – the merciless devils who would use him as a tool of propaganda."

The cheers grew louder. Once again Wyman raised his hands and the room fell silent. Campbell held back his laughter and, at the same time, felt his face heating up in embarrassment.

"Now, these here merciless devils, not being as smart as our fair-haired..." He paused and looked at Campbell closely.

Desert Fire

"Make that 'our dark-haired' hero, gave him the opportunity to locate the target with such pinpoint accuracy that the Allied Forces were able to bomb open the door to the building and allow the aforementioned hero to escape before blowing the rest of the establishment plumb to hell."

The cheering was getting out of hand. Campbell stood motionless and red-faced. Wyman raised his hands again. "Wait. There's more." Silence. "Our dark-haired hero sent a code so simple, we had to call in an expert code breaker from the Pentagon to crack it – with my expert help, of course."

"Of course!" said someone.

"Of course!" shouted the group in unison.

Wyman continued. "We are so fortunate to have said expert in our midst on this very day." He turned to the galley. "Mr. *First* Lieutenant Buzz Griswold, may I present to you and to my fellow hero worshipers, the one and only Captain Jim Campbell, Pride of the *Coral Sea*.

Buzz stepped out of the galley and moved stiffly to the front of Campbell, where he clicked his heels together smartly and saluted.

Campbell returned the salute crisply and the lieutenant dropped his hand sharply to his side.

"Welcome back, sir." He offered his hand.

"Thank you, Lieutenant. It's good to be here." Campbell smiled broadly.

Wyman jumped him first, hugging and squeezing him, but his solo didn't last long. Campbell was buried under an avalanche of bodies. After several moments of gasping for air and feeling the weight of too many bodies, Campbell was allowed to stand, his once-pressed Khaki uniform wrinkled and torn. He pushed his hand through his hair as he stood erect.

"I was just in more danger of being killed here than I was in Iraq."

Laughter erupted again, followed by an awkward silence.

Stoney Livingston

"It's good to have you back, Jim," said Redd.

Campbell wiped a tear from his eye. "It's good to be here, Jeff."

"Well, enough of this sentimental, maudlin bullshit," said Wyman. "How about some cake and beer?"

Campbell raised a hand. "How about we take this party to the hangar deck? I've got a few friends waiting for me up there. A recon team that saved my bacon in Khafji. I had to pull a lot of strings to get them here, especially the injured one."

"Grunts?" said Posner.

Campbell smiled. "Super grunts."

"What the hell are we waiting for?" said Wyman. He turned to Buzz. "Say, Lieutenant, see to it we have plenty of beer, will you? You ain't seen nothing until you see a grunt drink beer."

Desert Fire

CHAPTER 18

With the exception of Lugwrench, who lay on a stretcher, the rest of the recon team stood at attention near the fuselage of Wyman's F-18. The four North Vietnamese and one Iraqi flag below the canopy shouted out the major's victories in the air. The marines' camouflage utilities blended in with the war paint on the aircraft.

The group of fifteen or so officers approached the recon team warily, with respect. Campbell spoke first, "What the hell are you guys doing, standing at attention? At ease, goddamnit."

They relaxed and stood easy.

Campbell panned the infantrymen with his hand and spoke to the pilots, "These, gentlemen, are the heroes of Khafji." He faced Spanky and his men. "Gentlemen, may I present the misfits of VMI Three Sixty-Five."

The officers moved in and made their own personal introductions, handing out beer with each meeting. Shortly, the plane was surrounded by stools, benches and barrels, drawn up for seating. War stories were told and retold.

Early in the conversations, Smitty looked about the hangar deck, then back to Campbell. "You guys live like this all the time?"

Campbell smiled. "I'd like to bullshit you and say yes, but it's against regulations to smoke on the hangar deck, and Bob and Buzz smuggled the beer aboard yesterday."

"What happens if we get caught?"

"Nothing to you guys. You're just following orders. I'm ordering you to drink beer."

"Yessir!" Smitty took a big pull at his can of Carling.

Stoney Livingston

In the late afternoon, down to the last case of beer, most of the officers had quit drinking. This was the Three Sixty Fifth's night off, but you could never be certain of that in the Marine Corps. The recon team, with Spanky in the lead, continued to consume the beer at an amazing rate. All were in the advanced stages of intoxication, and all seemed to be maintaining a spirit of warmth and happiness.

Lugwrench was sound asleep in his cot, Smitty and Ski busy climbing in and out of Wyman's F-18, Obie deeply involved in a political discussion with Redd; Pup and Spanky learning the basics of combat flying from Posner. Wyman tapped Campbell on the shoulder.

"Let's drift to port for a second. Buzz here wants to talk to you about something."

Campbell looked into the flushed face of the young lieutenant. "You know, you remind me of a surfer. Except for that damn haircut. Why the hell you keep it cut so short? Looks too damn military."

"We *are* in the military."

"Good point. Damn good point." Campbell was feeling no pain. He joined them in a slow walk to a ladder leading topside. When they reached the railing on the flight deck, Wyman leaned into it.

"Jim, now that we're away from the crowd, I just wanted to say it's more than good to see you back. I knew you'd make it." He looked awkwardly out at the Persian Gulf, the water turned orange by the rays of the setting sun.

Campbell thought of his "execution". "Well, I'm glad someone had faith in something. Me, I'm just glad to be back." He punched Wyman lightly on the shoulder. "So tell me about the big number five."

Wyman stood away from the railing. "There's not much to tell. I never saw him eye to eye. It was all a big video game. Kind of takes something out of it, if you know what I mean?" He shrugged. "Anyway, it's done and over with. I got number five, and now it's time to look for another job."

"Me too, Bob. Me too. I asked the Old Man for a transfer today."

"You what?" Wyman's eyes were wide.

Campbell looked out to sea. "I don't know what I want anymore."

"Goddamnit, Jim, that's stupid. We all take our chances in this outfit. It could have been me or Mutt, or anybody else that got shot down."

"That doesn't matter to me, Bob. I'm not taking another F-18 into combat. I don't have to. Hell, it seems like I don't have to do much of anything. Some general wants me to take a speaking tour of the States, visit universities and talk about my experiences in Iraq. Can you believe that shit?"

"Captain Campbell."

Campbell turned to look at Buzz, who had remained silently in the background. He smiled warmly. "Don't be afraid of my rank, son. I'm here to help you." Campbell laughed at the old joke. "Hell, Buzz, the name is Jim. I was never cut out for this military shit anyway. I'm only here because I like to fly fast airplanes. The civilian models are too slow."

"Jim, I'd like to talk to you about your request for transfer."

"You got some pull in that direction?"

Buzz nodded. "I may have some. It just depends on what you request."

Campbell laughed. "I requested A-4s."

"Skyhawks?" asked Wyman.

Campbell nodded.

"Hell, the only ones flying the old hawks over here are the Free Kuwaiti Air Force pilots."

"Yeah, that's what the Old Man told me. And when I told him I didn't mind flying for them, he lost his damn sense of humor."

Stoney Livingston

"Have you ever considered intelligence work?" asked Buzz.

Campbell laughed. "Hell, I'm not intelligent enough for intelligence work. I think I've had enough of that spy stuff to last me a while. I'd rather hunt grizzlies with a willow switch."

Buzz had a serious expression on his face. "We need your talents, Jim."

"We? Who the hell is we?"

"Your country. The U.S. of A. Remember?"

"Oh, them." Campbell licked his lips. "I could sure use another beer."

Wyman said, "Just like that? The conversation with Buzz is over?"

Campbell looked at him sheepishly. "Hell, Bob, I thought I covered it pretty well. You ever hunt a grizz with a willow switch?"

"Think about it, Jim. Buzz's people have a temporary assignment for you if you want it. I don't even know what it is, but maybe if you took it, by the time it was over, you'd snap out of your cheap shit about flying the eighteens."

Campbell turned to face Buzz. "What the hell have you done to my buddy here? Brainwashed him? Look, Buzz, old man, I'd like to help, but . . .Oh shit, go ahead. Tell me what the hell it is. I'll listen. The least I can do, I guess."

Buzz looked over to Wyman and waited.

Wyman cleared his throat. "Listen, Jim, I'm gonna check on the grunts. We don't need Mutt or Jeff takin' 'em up for a ride right about now. I'll be right back."

"Yeah, well, you take care of them guys. Don't let anyone give 'em any shit." He thought of the injured Lugwrench and their decision to stay and fight to the death if need be. "Course I don't think it would benefit anybody on board if they tried it."

Wyman smiled and left them alone on deck. Campbell turned and looked Buzz squarely in the eyes. "So, Buzz, what's so damn secret that Bob Wyman can't even hear it?"

Buzz looked to his left and right. He moved a step closer to

Campbell. "You've got the background and training to do a job for us behind enemy lines. And you've got a memory that records exact details. We need your abilities."

"Behind enemy lines? Are you crazy? I just came from there, remember? I don't remember losing anything over there that's worth going back for." He thought of Zahra. *Well, there might be one thing.*

"You wouldn't be an escaped prisoner of war this time. You'll have identification and papers."

"Great. I'll be a damned spy. You know how long it takes them to decide to shoot a spy over there? Less than a New York minute – that's how long. And I don't speak Arabic. Let's forget that plan. What other jobs you got?"

"You won't have to speak Arabic. Your papers will identify you as a professor of mathematics from Switzerland. You speak fluent German."

Campbell nodded. "But what in the hell am I doing in Iraq?"

"We have a contact in Baghdad. She's in the English department of the University there. She's a member of the committee to find a math professor to run the math department."

Campbell thought again of Zahra. *Who knows? I might get to see her. She said she was an English teacher.* "How will I get into the country?"

Buzz smiled. "You jump."

"Oh shit. More of this secret mission stuff? Couldn't I just take a bus or something? And how will I explain how I got into the country?"

"You were in the country before the war started."

"I was?"

"Your passport will be stamped appropriately. You've been staying with friends of yours. A couple you met while vacationing in France last year – Kobar and Zobaydeh Jabar. He's in the banking business, a well-respected member of the government, and most importantly, a member of the resistance."

Stoney Livingston

"Why haven't I reported to the university sooner?"

"You've been afraid. Kobar has finally convinced you that it is safe, and that the university will make a choice on a department head soon. You have to get your name in the hat before it's too late."

"What information am I looking for?"

"A complete list of all the academicians we can count on to oppose Saddam Hussein when this thing is over. And the physical resources at Saddam's disposal to put down rebellion."

"Oh, that's all? I thought you were giving me a tough assignment. What the hell are you guys smoking anyway?"

"There's more."

"There's more? Oh good."

"We need to know his key people and what their functions are, and how they are authorized to carry them out."

"What kind of weapon do I carry?"

Buzz shook his head. "Sorry. No weapons."

"No weapons? *You're* sorry? I'm sorry as hell."

"This isn't the kind of assignment you can shoot your way out of if you are compromised."

"Compromised? Does that mean, 'discovered as a spy'? Why don't you just say 'found out'? Or maybe 'dead', or something more appropriate than 'compromised'? Jesus, Buzz, you been watchin' too many spy movies."

"If you're going to do it, we need to know right away. The timing is very important."

A slight breeze picked up and tossed Campbell's longer-than-regulation hair. He looked out to sea. He thought of his request for transfer. It would take a while to certify in another type aircraft. The war might be over by then and he would get out of the service anyway. If he took Buzz's offer, he might get to see Zahra again. He missed Akbar and Tahaleh too. They were good people – different – but good. Maybe he would learn the fate of Fatemeh and her husband.

Desert Fire

He put his back to the rail and studied Buzz. *How the hell does a guy that looks like everybody's picture of the All-American boy get a desk job breaking codes? He looks like he ought to be leading a rifle company up a ridge.*

"I parachute in, right?"

The End